EX LIBRIS

VINTAGE CLASSICS

THE SNOWS OF KILIMANJARO

Ernest Miller Hemingway was born in 1899. His father was a doctor and he was the second of six children. Their home was at Oak Park, a Chicago suburb.

In 1917 Hemingway joined the Kansas City *Star* as a cub reporter. The following year he volunteered to work as an ambulance driver on the Italian front where he was badly wounded but twice decorated for his services. He returned to America in 1919 and married in 1921. In 1922 he reported on the Greco-Turkish war, then two years later resigned from journalism to devote himself to fiction. He settled in Paris where he renewed his earlier friendship with such fellow-American expatriates as Ezra Pound and Gertrude Stein. Their encouragement and criticism were to play a valuable part in the formation of his style.

Hemingway's first two published works were *Three Stories and Ten Poems* and *In Our Time* but it was the satirical novel, *The Torrents of Spring*, that established his name more widely. His international reputation was firmly secured by his next three books: *Fiesta, Men Without Women* and *A Farewell to Arms*.

He was passionately involved with bullfighting, big-game hunting and deep-sea fishing, and his writing reflected this. He visited Spain during the Civil War and described his experiences in the bestseller, *For Whom the Bell Tolls*.

His direct and deceptively simple style of writing spawned generations of imitators but no equals. Recognition of his position in contemporary literature came in 1954 when he was awarded the Nobel Prize for Literature, following the publication of *The Old Man and the Sea*. He died in 1961.

ALSO BY ERNEST HEMINGWAY

Novels

The Torrents of Spring
Fiesta
A Farewell to Arms
To Have and Have Not
For Whom the Bell Tolls
Across the River and Into the Trees
The Old Man and the Sea
Islands in the Stream
The Garden of Eden
True at First Light

Stories

Men Without Women
Winner Take Nothing

General

Death in the Afternoon
Green Hills of Africa
A Moveable Feast
The Dangerous Summer

Drama

The Fifth Column

Collected Works

The Essential Hemingway
The First Forty-Nine Stories
By-Line

ERNEST HEMINGWAY

The Snows of Kilimanjaro

And Other Stories

VINTAGE BOOKS
London

Published by Vintage 2004

2 4 6 8 10 9 7 5 3 1

First published in the United Kingdom in *The Fifth Column* and
The First Forty-Nine (re-issued in 1944 as *The First Forty-Nine Stories*)
by Jonathan Cape in 1939

Vintage
Random House, 20 Vauxhall Bridge Road,
London SW1V 2SA

www.vintage-classics.info

Addresses for companies within The Random House Group Limited
can be found at: www.randomhouse.co.uk/offices.htm

The Random House Group Limited Reg. No. 954009

A CIP catalogue record for this book
is available from the British Library

ISBN 9780099595649

The Random House Group Limited supports The Forest Stewardship
Council® (FSC®), the leading international forest-certification
organisation. Our books carrying the FSC label are printed on
FSC®-certified paper. FSC is the only forest-certification scheme
supported by the leading environmental organisations, including
Greenpeace. Our paper procurement policy can be found at
www.randomhouse.co.uk/environment

Printed and bound in Great Britain by
CPI Group (UK) Ltd, Croydon, CR0 4YY

Contents

The Snows of Kilimanjaro

Kilimanjaro is a snow-covered mountain 19,710 feet high, and is said to be the highest mountain in Africa. Its western summit is called the Masai 'Ngàje Ngài', the House of God. Close to the western summit there is the dried and frozen carcass of a leopard. No one has explained what the leopard was seeking at that altitude.

'The marvellous thing is that it's painless,' he said. 'That's how you know when it starts.'

'Is it really?'

'Absolutely. I'm awfully sorry about the odour though. That must bother you.'

'Don't! Please don't.'

'Look at them,' he said. 'Now is it sight or is it scent that brings them like that?'

The cot the man lay on was in the wide shade of a mimosa tree and as he looked out past the shade on to the glare of the plain there were three of the big birds squatted obscenely, while in the sky a dozen more sailed, making quick-moving shadows as they passed.

'They've been there since the day the truck broke down,' he said. 'Today's the first time any have lit on the ground. I watched the way they sailed very carefully at first in case I ever wanted to use them in a story. That's funny now.'

'I wish you wouldn't,' she said.

'I'm only talking,' he said. 'It's much easier if I talk. But I don't want to bother you.'

'You know it doesn't bother me,' she said. 'It's that I've gotten so nervous not being able to do anything. I think we might make it as easy as we can until the plane comes.'

'Or until the plane doesn't come.'

'Please tell me what I can do. There must be something I can do.'

'You can take the leg off and that might stop it, though I doubt it. Or you can shoot me. You're a good shot now. I taught you to shoot didn't I?'

'Please don't talk that way. Couldn't I read to you?'

'Read what?'

'Anything in the book bag that we haven't read.'

'I can't listen to it,' he said. 'Talking is easier. We quarrel and that makes the time pass.'

'We don't quarrel. I never want to quarrel. Let's not quarrel any more. No matter how nervous we get. Maybe they will be back with another truck. Maybe the plane will come.'

'I don't want to move,' the man said. 'There is no sense in moving now except to make it easier for you.'

'That's cowardly.'

'Can you let a man die as comfortably as he can without calling him names? What's the use of slanging me?'

'You're not going to die.'

'Don't be silly. I'm dying now. Ask those bastards.' He looked over to where the huge, filthy birds sat, their naked heads sunk in the hunched feathers. A fourth planed down to run quick-legged and then waddle slowly toward the others.

'They are around every camp. You never notice them. You can't die if you don't give up.'

'Where did you read that? You're such a bloody fool.'

'You might think about someone else.'

'For Christ's sake,' he said. 'That's been my trade.'

He lay then and was quiet for a while and looked across the heat shimmer of the plain to the edge of the bush. There were a few Tommies that showed minute and white against the yellow and, far off, he saw a herd of zebra, white against the green of the bush. This was a pleasant camp under big trees against a hill, with good water, and close by, a nearly dry water hole where sand grouse flighted in the mornings.

'Wouldn't you like me to read?' she asked. She was sitting on a canvas chair beside his cot. 'There's a breeze coming up.'

'No thanks.'

'Maybe the truck will come.'

'I don't give a damn about the truck.'

'I do.'

'You give a damn about so many things that I don't.'

'Not so many, Harry.'

'What about a drink?'

'It's supposed to be bad for you. It said in Black's to avoid all alcohol. You shouldn't drink.'

'Molo!' he shouted.

'Yes Bwana.'

'Bring whisky-soda.'

'Yes Bwana.'

'You shouldn't,' she said. 'That's what I mean by giving up. It says it's bad for you. I know it's bad for you.'

'No,' he said. 'It's good for me.'

So now it was all over, he thought. So now he would never have a chance to finish it. So this was the way it ended in a bickering over a drink. Since the gangrene started in his right leg he had no pain and with the pain the horror had gone and all he felt now was a great tiredness and anger that this was the end of it. For years, that now was coming, he had very little curiosity. For years it had obsessed him; but now it meant nothing in itself. It was strange how easy being tired enough made it.

Now he would never write the things that he had saved to write until he knew enough to write them well. Well, he would not have to fail at trying to write them either. Maybe you would not have to fail at trying to write them either. Maybe you could never write them, and that was why you put them off and delayed the starting. Well he would never know, now.

'I wish we'd never come,' the woman said. She was looking at him holding the glass and biting her lip. 'You never would have gotten anything like this in Paris. You always said you loved Paris. We could have stayed in Paris or gone anywhere. I'd have gone anywhere. I said I'd go anywhere you wanted. If you wanted to shoot we could have gone shooting in Hungary and been comfortable.'

'Your bloody money,' he said.

'That's not fair,' she said. 'It was always yours as much as mine. I left everything and I went wherever you wanted to go and I've done what you wanted to do. But I wish we'd never come here.'

'You said you loved it.'

'I did when you were all right. But now I hate it. I don't see why that had to happen to your leg. What have we done to have that happen to us?'

'I suppose what I did was to forget to put iodine on it when I first scratched it. Then I didn't pay any attention to it because I never infect. Then, later, when it got bad, it was probably using that weak carbolic solution when the other antiseptics ran out that paralysed the minute blood vessels and started the gangrene.' He looked at her. 'What else?'

'I don't mean that.'

'If we would have hired a good mechanic instead of a half-baked kikuyu driver, he would have checked the oil and never burned out that bearing in the truck.'

'I don't mean that.'

'If you hadn't left your own people, your goddamned Old Westbury, Saratoga, Palm Beach people to take me on—'

'Why, I loved you. That's not fair. I love you now. I'll always love you. Don't you love me?'

'No,' said the man. 'I don't think so. I never have.'

'Harry, what are you saying? You're out of your head.'

'No. I haven't any head to go out of.'

'Don't drink that,' she said. 'Darling, please don't drink that. We have to do everything we can.'

'You do it,' he said. 'I'm tired.'

Now in his mind he saw a railway station at Karagatch and he was standing with his pack and that was the headlight of the Simplon–Orient cutting the dark now and he was leaving Thrace then after the retreat. That was one of the things he had saved to write, with, in the morning at breakfast, looking out the window and seeing snow on the mountains in Bulgaria and Nansen's Secretary asking the old man if it were snow and the old man

4

looking at it and saying, No, that's not snow. It's too early for snow. And the Secretary repeating to the other girls, No, you see. It's not snow and them all saying, It's not snow we were mistaken. But it was snow all right and he sent them on into it when he evolved exchange of populations. And it was snow they trampled along in until they died that winter.

It was snow too that fell all Christmas week that year up in the Gauertal, that year they lived in the woodcutter's house with the big square porcelain stove that filled half the room, and they slept on mattresses filled with beech leaves, the time the deserter came with his feet bloody in the snow. He said the police were right behind him and they gave him woollen socks and held the gendarmes talking until the tracks had drifted over.

In Schrunz, on Christmas day, the snow was so bright it hurt your eyes when you looked out from the weinstube and saw everyone coming home from church. That was where they walked up the sleigh-smoothed urine-yellowed road along the river with the steep pine hills, skis heavy on the shoulder, and where they mean that great run down the glacier above the Madlener-Haus, the snow as smooth to see as a cake frosting and as light as powder and he remembered the noiseless rush the speed made as you dropped down like a bird.

They were snow-bound a week later in the Madlener-Haus that time in the blizzard playing cards in the smoke by the lantern light and the stakes were higher all the time as Herr Lent lost more. Finally he lost it all. Everything, the skischule money and all the season's profit and then his capital. He could see him with his long nose, picking up the cards and then opening, 'Sans Voir'. There was always gambling then. When there was no snow you gambled and when there was too much you gambled. He thought of all the time in his life he had spent gambling.

But he had never written a line of that, nor of that cold, bright Christmas day with the mountains showing across the plain that Barker had flown across the lines to bomb the Austrian officers' leave train, machine-gunning them as they scattered and ran. He remembered Barker afterwards coming into the mess and starting to tell about it. And how quiet it got and then somebody saying, 'You bloody murderous bastard.'

Those were the same Austrians they killed then that he skied with later. No, not the same. Hans, that he skied with all that year, had been in the Kaiser-Jägers and when they went hunting hares together up the little valley above the saw-mill they had talked of the fighting on Pasubio and of the attack on Pertica and Asalone and he had never written a word of that. Nor of Monte Corno, nor the Siete Commun, nor of Arsiedo.

How many winters had he lived in the Vorarlberg and the Arlberg? It was four and then he remembered the man who had the fox to sell when they had walked into Bludenz, that time to buy presents, and the cherry-pit taste of good kirsch, the fast-slipping rush of running powder-snow on crust, singing 'Hi! Ho! Said Rolly!' as you ran down the last stretch to the steep drop, taking it straight, then running the orchard in three turns and out across the ditch and on to the icy road behind the inn. Knocking your bindings loose, kicking the skis free and leaning them up against the wooden wall of the inn, the lamp-light coming from the window, where inside, in the smoky, new-wine smelling warmth, they were playing the accordion.

'Where did we stay in Paris?' he asked the woman who was sitting by him in a canvas chair, now, in Africa.

'At the Crillon. You know that.'

'Why do I know that?'

'That's where we always stayed.'

'No. Not always.'

'There and at the Pavillon Henri-Quatre in St Germain. You said you loved it there.'

'Love in a dunghill,' said Harry. 'And I'm the cock that gets on it to crow.'

'If you have to go away,' she said, 'is it absolutely necessary to kill off everything you leave behind? I mean do you have to take away everything. Do you have to kill your horse, and your wife and burn your saddle and your armour?'

'Yes,' he said. 'Your damned money was my armour. My Swift and my Armour.'

'Don't.'

'All right. I'll stop that. I don't want to hurt you.'

'It's a little bit late now.'

6

'All right then. I'll go on hurting you. It's more amusing. The only thing I ever really liked to do with you I can't do now.'

'No, that's not true. You liked to do many things and everything you wanted to do I did.'

'Oh, for Christ's sake stop bragging, will you?'

He looked at her and saw her crying.

'Listen,' he said. 'Do you think that it is fun to do this? I don't know why I'm doing it. It's trying to kill to keep yourself alive, I imagine. I was all right when we started talking. I didn't mean to start this, and now I'm crazy as a coot and being as cruel to you as I can be. Don't pay attention, darling, to what I say. I love you, really. You know I love you. I've never loved anyone else the way I love you.'

He slipped into the familiar lie he made his bread and butter by.

'You're sweet to me.'

'You bitch,' he said. 'You rich bitch. That's poetry. I'm full of poetry now. Rot and poetry. Rotten poetry.'

'Stop it. Harry, why do you have to turn into a devil now?'

'I don't have to leave anything,' the man said. 'I don't like to leave things behind.'

It was evening now and he had been asleep. The sun was gone behind the hill and there was a shadow all across the plain and the small animals were feeding close to camp; quick dropping heads and switching tails, he watched them keeping well out away from the bush now. The birds no longer waited on the ground. They were all perched heavily in a tree. There were many more of them. His personal boy was sitting by the bed.

'Memsahib's gone to shoot,' the boy said. 'Does Bwana want?'

'Nothing.'

She had gone to kill a piece of meat and, knowing how he liked to watch the game, she had gone well away so she would disturb this little pocket of the plain that he could see. She was always thoughtful, he thought. On anything she knew about, or had read, or that she had ever heard.

It was not her fault that when he went to her he was already over. How could a woman know that you meant nothing that you said; that you spoke only from habit and to be comfortable? After he no longer meant what he said, his lies were more successful with women than when he had told them the truth.

It was not so much that he lied as that there was no truth to tell. He had had his life and it was over and then he went on living it again with different people and more money, with the best of the same places, and some new ones.

You kept from thinking and it was all marvellous. You were equipped with good insides so that you did not go to pieces that way, the way most of them had, and you made an attitude that you cared nothing for the work you used to do, now that you could no longer do it. But, in yourself, you said that you would write about these people; about the very rich; that you were really not of them but a spy in their country; that you would leave it and write of it and for once it would be written by someone who knew what he was writing of. But he would never do it, because each day of not writing, of comfort, of being that which he despised, dulled his ability and softened his will to work so that, finally, he did no work at all. The people he knew now were all much more comfortable when he did not work. Africa was where he had been happiest in the good time of his life, so he had come out here to start again. They had made this safari with the minimum of comfort. There was no hardship; but there was no luxury and he had thought that he could get back into training that way. That in some way he could work the fat off his soul the way a fighter went into the mountains to work and train in order to burn it out of his body.

She had liked it. She said she loved it. She loved anything that was exciting, that involved a change of scene, where there were new people and where things were pleasant. And he had felt the illusion of returning strength of will to work. Now if this was how it ended, and he knew it was, he must not turn like some snake biting itself because its back was broken. It wasn't this woman's fault. If it had not been she it would have been another. If he lived by a lie he should try to die by it. He heard a shot beyond the hill.

She shot very well this good, this rich bitch, this kindly caretaker and destroyer of his talent. Nonsense. He had destroyed his talent himself. Why should he blame this woman because she kept him well? He had destroyed his talent by not using it, by betrayals of himself and what he believed in, by drinking so much that he blunted the edge of his perceptions, by laziness, by sloth, and by snobbery, by pride and by prejudice, by hook and by crook. What was this? A catalogue of old books? What was his talent anyway? It was a talent all right but instead of using it, he had traded on it. It was never what he had done, but always what he could do. And he had chosen to make his living with something else instead of a pen or a pencil. It was strange, too, wasn't it, that when he fell in love with another woman, that woman should always have more money than the last one? But when he no longer was in love, when he was only lying, as to this woman, now, who had the most money of all, who had all the money there was, who had had a husband and children, who had taken lovers and been dissatisfied with them, and who loved him dearly as a writer, as a man, as a companion and as a proud possession; it was strange that he should be able to give her more for her money than when he had really loved.

We must all be cut out for what we do, he thought. However you make your living is where your talent lies. He had sold vitality, in one form or another, all his life and when your affections are not too involved you give much better value for the money. He had found that out but he would never write that, now, either. No, he would not write that, although it was well worth writing.

Now she came in sight, walking across the open toward the camp. She was wearing jodhpurs and carrying her rifle. The two boys had a Tommy slung and they were coming along behind her. She was still a good-looking woman, he thought, and she had a pleasant body. She had a great talent and appreciation for the bed, she was not pretty, but he liked her face, she read enormously, liked to ride and shoot and, certainly, she drank too much. Her husband had died when she was still a comparatively young woman and for a while she had devoted herself to her two just-grown children, who did not need her and were embarrassed at having her about, to her stable of horses, to books, and to bottles. She liked to read in the evening before dinner and she drank Scotch and soda while she read. By dinner she was fairly drunk and after a bottle of wine at dinner she was usually drunk enough to sleep.

That was before the lovers. After she had the lovers she did not drink so much because she did not have to be drunk to sleep. But the lovers bored her. She had been married to a man who had never bored her and these people bored her very much.

Then one of her two children was killed in a plane crash and after that was over she did not want the lovers, and drink being no anaesthetic she had to make another life. Suddenly, she had been acutely frightened of being alone. But she wanted someone that she respected with her.

It had begun very simply. She liked what he wrote and she had always envied the life he led. She thought he did exactly what he wanted to. The steps by which she had acquired him and the way in which she had finally fallen in love with him were all part of a regular progression in which she had built herself a new life and he had traded away what remained of his old life.

He had traded it for security, for comfort too, there was no denying that, and for what else? He did not know. She would have bought him anything he wanted. He knew that. She was a damned nice woman too. He would as soon be in bed with her as anyone; rather with her, because she was richer, because she was very pleasant and appreciative and because she never made scenes. And now this life that she had built again was coming to a term because he had not used iodine two weeks ago when a thorn had scratched his knee as they moved forward trying to photograph a herd of waterbuck standing, their heads up, peering while their nostrils searched the air, their ears spread wide to hear the first noise that would send them rushing into the bush. They had bolted, too, before he got the picture.

Here she came now.

He turned his head on the cot to look toward her. 'Hello,' he said.

'I shot a Tommy ram,' she told him. 'He'll make you a good broth and I'll have them mash some potatoes with the Klim. How do you feel?'

'Much better.'

'Isn't that lovely? You know I thought perhaps you would. You were sleeping when I left.'

'I had a good sleep. Did you walk far?'

'No. Just around behind the hill. I made quite a good shot on the Tommy.'

'You shoot marvellously, you know.'

'I love it. I've loved Africa. Really. If *you're* all right it's the most fun that I've ever had. You don't know the fun it's been to shoot with you. I've loved the country.'

'I love it too.'

'Darling, you don't know how marvellous it is to see you feeling better. I couldn't stand it when you felt that way. You won't talk to me like that again, will you? Promise me?'

'No,' he said. 'I don't remember what I said.'

'You don't have to destroy me. Do you? I'm only a middle-aged woman who loves you and wants to do what you want to do. I've been destroyed two or three times already. You wouldn't want to destroy me again, would you?'

'I'd like to destroy you a few times in bed,' he said.

'Yes. That's the good destruction. That's the way we're made to be destroyed. The plane will be here tomorrow.'

'How do you know?'

'I'm sure. It's bound to come. The boys have the wood all ready and the grass to make the smudge. I went down and looked at it again today. There's plenty of room to land and we have the smudgers ready at both ends.'

'What makes you think it will come tomorrow?'

'I'm sure it will. It's overdue now. Then, in town, they will fix up your leg and then we will have some good destruction. Not that dreadful talking kind.'

'Should we have a drink? The sun is down.'

'Do you think you should?'

'I'm having one.'

'We'll have one together. *Molo, letti dui whisky-soda!*' she called.

11

'You'd better put on your mosquito boots,' he told her.

'I'll wait till I bathe . . .'

While it grew dark they drank and just before it was dark and there was no longer enough light to shoot, a hyena crossed the open on his way around the hill.

'That bastard crosses there every night,' the man said. 'Every night for two weeks.'

'He's the one makes the noise at night. I don't mind it. They're a filthy animal though.'

Drinking together, with no pain now except the discomfort of lying in one position, the boys lighting a fire, its shadow jumping on the tents, he could feel the return of acquiescence in this life of pleasant surrender. She *was* very good to him. He had been cruel and unjust in the afternoon. She was a fine woman, marvellous really. And just then it occurred to him that he was going to die.

It came with a rush; not as a rush of water nor of wind; but of a sudden evil-smelling emptiness and the odd thing was that the hyena slipped lightly along the edge of it.

'What is it, Harry?' she asked him.

'Nothing,' he said. 'You had better move over to the other side. To windward.'

'Did Molo change the dressing?'

'Yes. I'm just feeling the boric now.'

'How do you feel?'

'A little wobbly.'

'I'm going in to bathe,' she said. 'I'll be right out. I'll eat with you and then we'll put the cot in.'

So, he said to himself, we did well to stop the quarrelling. He had never quarrelled much with this woman, while with the women that he loved he had quarrelled so much they had finally, always, with the corrosion of the quarrelling, killed what they had together. He had loved too much, demanded too much, and he wore it all out.

He thought about alone in Constantinople that time, having quarrelled in Paris before he had gone out. He had whored the whole time and then, when that was over, he had failed to kill his loneliness, but only made it worse, he had written her, the first one, the one who left him, a letter telling her how he had never been able to kill it . . . How when he thought he saw her outside the Regence one time it made him go all faint and sick inside, and that he would follow a woman who looked like her in some way, along the Boulevard, afraid to see it was not she, afraid to lose the feeling it gave him. How everyone he had slept with had only made him miss her more. How what she had done could never matter since he knew he could not cure himself of loving her. He wrote this letter at the Club, cold sober, and mailed it to New York asking her to write him at the office in Paris. That seemed safe. And that night missing her so much it made him feel hollow sick inside, he wandered up past Taxim's, picked a girl up and took her out to supper. He had gone to a place to dance with her afterwards, she danced badly, and left her for a hot American slut, that swung her belly against him so it almost scalded. He took her away from a British gunner subaltern after a row. The gunner asked him outside and they fought in the street on the cobbles in the dark. He'd hit him twice, hard, on the side of the jaw and when he didn't go down he knew he was in for a fight. The gunner hit him in the body, then beside his eye. He swung with his left again and landed and the gunner fell on him and grabbed his coat and tore the sleeve off and he clubbed him twice behind the ear and smashed him with his right as he pushed him away. When the gunner went down his head hit first and he ran with the girl because they heard the M.P.s coming. They got into a taxi and drove out to Rimmily Hissa along the Bosphorus, and around, and back in the cool night and went to bed and she felt as over-ripe as she looked but smooth, rose-petal, syrupy, smooth-bellied, big-breasted and needed no pillow under her buttocks, and he left her before she was awake looking blousy enough in the first daylight and turned up at the Pera Palace with a black eye, carrying his coat because one sleeve was missing.

The same night he left for Anatolia and he remembered, later on that trip, riding all day through fields of the poppies that they raised for opium and how strange it made you feel, finally, and all the distances seemed wrong, to where they had made the attack with the newly arrived Constantine officers, that did not know a goddamned thing, and the artillery had fired into the troops and the British observer had cried like a child.

That was the day he'd first seen dead men wearing white ballet skirts and upturned shoes with pompons on them. The Turks had come steadily and lumpily and he had seen the skirted men running and the officers shooting into them and running then themselves and he and the British observer had run too until his lungs ached and his mouth was full of the taste of pennies and they stopped behind some rocks and there were the Turks coming as lumpily as ever. Later he had seen the things that he could never think of and later still he had seen much worse. So when he got back to Paris that time he could not talk about it or stand to have it mentioned. And there in the café as he passed was that American poet with a pile of saucers in front of him and a stupid look on his potato face talking about the Dada movement with a Roumanian who said his name was Tristan Tzara, who always wore a monocle and had a headache, and, back at the apartment with his wife that now he loved again, the quarrel was over, the madness all over, glad to be home, the office sent his mail up to the flat. So then the letter in answer to the one he'd written came in on a platter one morning and when he saw the handwriting he went cold all over and tried to slip the letter underneath another. But his wife said, 'Who is that letter from, dear?' and that was the end of the beginning of that.

He remembered the good times with them all, and the quarrels. They always picked the finest places to have the quarrels. And why had they always quarrelled when he was feeling best? He had never written any of that because, at first, he never wanted to hurt anyone and then it seemed as though there was enough to write without it. But he had always thought that he would write it finally. There was so much to write. He had seen the world change; not just the events; although he had seen many of them and he could remember how the people were at different times. He had been in it and he had watched it and it was his duty to write of it; but now he never would.

'How do you feel?' she said. She had come out from the tent now after her bath.

'All right.'

'Could you eat now?' He saw Molo behind her with the

folding table and the other boy with the dishes.

'I want to write,' he said.

'You ought to take some broth to keep your strength up.'

'I'm going to die tonight,' he said. 'I don't need my strength up.'

'Don't be melodramatic, Harry, please,' she said.

'Why don't you use your nose? I'm rotted half-way up my thigh now. What the hell should I fool with broth for? Molo, bring whisky-soda.'

'Please take the broth,' she said gently.

'All right.'

The broth was too hot. He had to hold it in the cup until it cooled enough to take it and then he just got it down without gagging.

'You're a fine woman,' he said. 'Don't pay any attention to me.'

She looked at him with her well-known, well-loved face from *Spur* and *Town and Country*, only a little the worse for drink, only a little the worse for bed, but *Town and Country* never showed those good breasts and those useful thighs and those lightly small-of-back caressing hands, and as he looked and saw her well-known pleasant smile, he felt death come again. This time there was no rush. It was a puff, as of a wind that makes a candle flicker and the flame go tall.

'They can bring my net out later and hang it from the tree and build the fire up. I'm not going in the tent tonight. It's not worth moving. It's a clear night. There won't be any rain.'

So this was how you died, in whispers that you did not hear. Well, there would be no more quarrelling. He could promise that. The only experience that he had never had he was not going to spoil now. He probably would. You spoiled everything. But perhaps he wouldn't.

'You can't learn dictation, can you?'

'I never learned,' she told him.

'That's all right.'

There wasn't time, of course, although it seemed as though it telescoped so that you might put it all into one paragraph if you could get it right.

*

15

There was a log house, chinked white with mortar, on a hill above the lake. There was a bell on a pole by the door to call the people in to meals. Behind the house were fields and behind the fields was the timber. A line of lombardy poplars ran from the house to the dock. Other poplars ran along the point. A road went up to the hills along the edge of the timber and along that road he picked blackberries. Then that log house was burned down and all the guns that had been on deer foot racks above the open fireplace were burned and afterwards their barrels, with the lead melted in the magazines, and the stocks burned away, lay out on the heap of ashes that were being used to make lye for the big iron soap kettles, and you asked Grandfather if you could have them to play with, and he said, no. You see they were his guns still and he never bought any others. Nor did he hunt any more. The house was rebuilt in the same place out of lumber now and painted white and from its porch you saw poplars and the lake beyond; but there were never any more guns. The barrels of the guns that had hung on the deer feet on the wall of the log house lay out there on the heap of ashes and no one touched them.

In the Black Forest, after the war, we rented a trout stream and there were two ways to walk to it. One was down the valley from Triberg and around the valley road in the shade of the trees that bordered the white road, and then up a side road that went up through the hills, past many small farms, with the big Schwarzwald houses, until that road crossed the stream. That was where our fishing began.

The other way was to climb steeply up to the edge of the woods and then go across the top of the hills through the pine woods, and then out to the edge of a meadow and down across this meadow to the bridge. There were birches along the stream and it was not big, but narrow, clear and fast, with pools where it had cut under the roots of the birches. At the Hotel in Triberg the proprietor had a fine season. It was very pleasant and we were all great friends. The next year came the inflation and the money he had made the year before was not enough to buy supplies to open the hotel and he hanged himself.

You could dictate that, but you could not dictate the Place Contrescarpe where the flower sellers dyed their flowers in the street and the dye ran over the paving where the autobus started and the old men and the women, always drunk on wine and bad marc; and the children with their noses running in the cold; the smell of dirty sweat and poverty and drunkenness at the Café des Amateurs and the whores at the Bal Musette they lived above. The Concierge who entertained the trooper of the Garde Républicaine in her loge, his horse-hair-plumed helmet on a chair. The locataire across the hall whose husband was a bicycle racer and her joy that morning at the Crémerie when she had opened L'Auto and seen where he placed third in Paris-Tours, his first big race. She had blushed and laughed and then gone upstairs crying with the yellow sporting paper in her hand. The husband of the woman who ran the Bal Musette drove a taxi and when he, Harry, had to take an early plane the husband knocked upon the door to wake him and they each drank a glass of white wine at the zinc of the bar before they started. He knew his neighbours in that quarter then because they were all poor.

Around the Place there were two kinds; the drunkards and the sportifs. The drunkards killed their poverty that way; the sportifs took it out in exercise. They were the descendants of the Communards and it was no struggle for them to know their politics. They knew who had shot their fathers, their relatives, their brothers, and their friends when the Versailles troops came in and took the town after the Commune and executed anyone they could catch with calloused hands, or who wore a cap, or carried any other sign he was a working man. And in that poverty, and in that quarter across the street from a Boucherie Chevaline and a wine co-operative he had written the start of all he was to do. There was never another part of Paris that he loved like that, the sprawling trees, the old white plastered houses painted brown below, the long green of the autobus in that round square, the purple flower dye upon the paving, the sudden drop down the hill of the rue Cardinal Lemoine to the River, and the other way the narrow crowded world of the rue Mouffetard. The street that ran up towards the Panthéon and the other that he always took with the bicycle, the only asphalted street in all that quarter, smooth under the tyres, with the high narrow houses and the cheap tall hotel where Paul Verlain had died. There were only two rooms in the apartments where they lived and he had a room on the top floor of that hotel that cost him sixty francs a month where he did *his writing, and from it he could see the roofs and chimney pots and all the hills of Paris.*

From the apartment you could only see the wood and coal man's place. He sold wine too, bad wine. The golden horse's head outside the Boucherie Chevaline where the carcasses hung yellow gold and red in the open window, and the green painted co-operative where they bought their wine; good wine and cheap. The rest was plaster walls and the windows of the neighbours. The neighbours who, at night, when someone lay drunk in the street, moaning and groaning in that typical French ivresse that you were propaganded to believe did not exist, would open their windows and then the murmur of talk.

'Where is the policeman? When you don't want him the bugger is always there. He's sleeping with some concierge. Get the Agent.' Till someone threw a bucket of water from a window and the moaning stopped. 'What's that? Water. Ah, that's intelligent.' And the windows shutting. Marie, his femme de ménage, protesting against the eight-hour day saying, 'If a husband works until six he gets only a little drunk on the way home and does not waste too much. If he works only until five he is drunk every night and one has no money. It is the wife of the working man who suffers from this shortening of hours.'

'Wouldn't you like some more broth?' the woman asked now.

'No, thank you very much. It is awfully good.'

'Try just a little.'

'I would like a whisky-soda.'

'It's not good for you.'

'No. It's bad for me. Cole Porter wrote the words and the music. This knowledge that you're going mad for me.'

'You know I like you to drink.'

'Oh yes. Only it's bad for me.'

When she goes, he thought, I'll have all I want. Not all I want but all there is. Ayee he was tired. Too tired. He was going to sleep a little while. He lay still and death was not there. It must have gone around another street. It went in pairs, on bicycles, and moved absolutely silently on the pavements.

No, he had never written about Paris. Not the Paris that he cared about. But what about the rest that he had never written?

What about the ranch and the silvered grey of the sage brush, the quick, clear water in the irrigation ditches, and the heavy green of the alfalfa. The trail went up into the hills and the cattle in the summer were as shy as deer. The bawling and the steady noise and slow moving mass raising a dust as you brought them down in the fall. And behind the mountains, the clear sharpness of the peak in the evening light and, riding down along the trail in the moonlight, bright across the valley. Now he remembered coming down through the timber in the dark holding the horse's tail when you could not see and all the stories that he meant to write.

About the half-wit chore boy who was left at the ranch that time and told not to let anyone get any hay, and that old bastard from the Forks who had beaten the boy when he had worked for him stopping to get some feed. The boy refusing and the old man saying he would beat him again. The boy got the rifle from the kitchen and shot him when he tried to come into the barn and when they came back to the ranch he'd been dead a week, frozen in the corral, and the dogs had eaten part of him. But what was left you packed on a sled wrapped in a blanket and roped on and you got the boy to help you haul it, and the two of you took it out over the road on skis, and sixty miles down to town to turn the boy over. He having no idea that he would be arrested. Thinking he had done his duty and that you were his friend and he would be rewarded. He'd helped to haul the old man in so everybody could know how bad the old man had been and how he'd tried to steal some food that didn't belong to him, and when the sheriff put the hand-cuffs on the boy he couldn't believe it. Then he'd started to cry. That was one story he had saved to write. He knew at least twenty good stories from out there and he had never written one. Why?

'You tell them why,' he said.

'Why what, dear?'

'Why nothing.'

She didn't drink so much, now, since she had him. But if he

lived he would never write about her, he knew that now. Nor about any of them. The rich were dull and they drank too much, or they played too much backgammon. They were dull and they were repetitious. He remembered poor Julian and his romantic awe of them and how he had started a story once that began, 'The very rich are different from you and me.' And how someone had said to Julian, Yes, they have more money. But that was not humorous to Julian. He thought they were a special glamorous race and when he found they weren't it wrecked him just as much as any other thing that wrecked him.

He had been contemptuous of those who wrecked. You did not have to like it because you understood it. He could beat anything, he thought, because nothing could hurt him if he did not care.

All right. Now he would not care for death. One thing he had always dreaded was the pain. He could stand pain as well as any man, until it went on too long, and wore him out, but here he had something that had hurt frightfully and just when he had felt it breaking him, the pain stopped.

He remembered long ago when Williamson, the bombing officer, had been hit by a stick bomb someone in a German patrol had thrown as he was coming in through the wire that night and, screaming, had begged everyone to kill him. He was a fat man, very brave, and a good officer, although addicted to fantastic shows. But that night he was caught in the wire, with a flare lighting him up and his bowels spilled out into the wire, so when they brought him in, alive, they had to cut him loose. Shoot me, Harry. For Christ sake shoot me. They had had an argument one time about our Lord never sending you anything you could not bear and someone's theory had been that meant that at a certain time the pain passed you out automatically. But he had always remembered Williamson, that night. Nothing passed out Williamson until he gave him all his morphine tablets that he had always saved to use himself and then they did not work right away.

Still this now, that he had, was very easy; and if it was no worse

20

as it went on there was nothing to worry about. Except that he would rather be in better company.

He thought a little about the company that he would like to have.

No, he thought, when everything you do, you do too long, and do too late, you can't expect to find the people still there. The people are all gone. The party's over and you are with your hostess now.

I'm getting as bored with dying as with everything else, he thought.

'It's a bore,' he said out loud.

'What is, my dear?'

'Anything you do too bloody long.'

He looked at her face between him and the fire. She was leaning back in the chair and the firelight shone on her pleasantly lined face and he could see that she was sleepy. He heard the hyena make a noise just outside the range of the fire.

'I've been writing,' he said. 'But I got tired.'

'Do you think you will be able to sleep?'

'Pretty sure. Why don't you turn in?'

'I like to sit here with you.'

'Do you feel anything strange?' he asked her.

'No. Just a little sleepy.'

'I do,' he said.

He had just felt death come by again.

'You know the only thing I've never lost is curiosity,' he said to her.

'You've never lost anything. You're the most complete man I've ever known.'

'Christ,' he said. 'How little a woman knows. What is that? Your intuition?'

Because, just then, death had come and rested its head on the foot of the cot and he could smell its breath.

'Never believe any of that about a scythe and a skull,' he told her. 'It can be two bicycle policemen as easily, or a bird. Or it can have a wide snout like a hyena.'

It had moved up on him now, but it had no shape any more. It simply occupied space.

'Tell it to go away.'

21

It did not go away but moved a little closer.

'You've got a hell of a breath,' he told her. 'You stinking bastard.'

It moved up closer to him still and now he could not speak to it, and when it saw he could not speak it came a little closer, and now he tried to send it away without speaking, but it moved in on him so its weight was all upon his chest, and while it crouched there and he could not move, or speak, he heard the woman say, 'Bwana is asleep now. Take the cot up very gently and carry it into the tent.'

He could not speak to tell her to make it go away and it crouched now, heavier, so he could not breathe. And then, while they lifted the cot, suddenly it was all right and the weight went from his chest.

It was morning and had been morning for some time and he heard the plane. It showed very tiny and then made a wide circle and the boys ran out and lit the fires, using kerosene and piled on grass so there were two big smudges at each end of the level place and the morning breeze blew them toward the camp and the plane circled twice more, low this time, and then glided down and levelled off and landed smoothly and, coming walking toward him, was old Compton in slacks, a tweed jacket and a brown felt hat.

'What's the matter, old cock?' Compton said.

'Bad leg,' he told him. 'Will you have some breakfast?'

'Thanks. I'll just have some tea. It's the Puss Moth, you know. I won't be able to take the Memsahib. There's only room for one. Your lorry is on the way.'

Helen had taken Compton aside and was speaking to him. Compton came back more cheery than ever.

'We'll get you right in,' he said. 'I'll be back for the Mem. Now I'm afraid I'll have to stop at Arusha to refuel. We'd better get going.'

'What about the tea?'

'I don't really care about it, you know.'

The boys had picked up the cot and carried it around the green tents and down along the rock and out on to the plain and along past the smudges that were burning brightly now, the grass all consumed, and the wind fanning the fire, to the little plane. It was difficult getting him in, but once he lay back in the leather seat, and the leg was stuck straight out to one side of the seat where Compton sat. Compton started the motor and got in. He waved to Helen and to the boys and, as the clatter moved into the old familiar roar, they swung around with Compie watching for wart-hog holes and roared, bumping, along the stretch between the fires and with the last bump rose and he saw them all standing below, waving, and the camp beside the hill, flattening now, and the plain spreading, clumps of trees, and the bush flattening, while the game trails ran now smoothly to the dry waterholes, and there was a new water that he had never known of. The zebra, small rounded backs now, and the wildebeeste, big-headed dots seeming to climb as they moved in long fingers across the plain, now scattering as the shadow came toward them, they were tiny now, and the movement had no gallop, and the plain as far as you could see, grey-yellow now and ahead old Compie's tweed back and the brown felt hat. Then they were over the first hills and the wildebeeste were trailing up them, and then they were over mountains with sudden depths of green-rising forest and the solid bamboo slopes, and then the heavy forest again, sculpted into peaks and hollows until they crossed, and hills sloped down and then another plain, hot now, and purple brown, bumpy with heat and Compie looking back to see how he was riding. Then there were other mountains dark ahead.

And then instead of going on to Arusha they turned left, he evidently figured that they had the gas, and looking down he saw a pink sifting cloud, moving over the ground, and in the air, like the first snow in a blizzard, that comes from nowhere, and he knew the locusts were coming up from the South. Then they began to climb and they were going to the East it seemed, and then it darkened and they were in a storm, the rain so thick it seemed like flying through a waterfall, and then they were out and Compie turned his head and grinned and pointed and there, ahead, all he could see, as wide as all the world, great, high, and unbelievably white in the sun, was the top of Kilimanjaro. And then he knew that there was where he was going.

23

Just then the hyena stopped whimpering in the night and started to make a strange, human, almost crying sound. The woman heard it and stirred uneasily. She did not wake. In her dream she was at the house on Long Island and it was the night before her daughter's debut. Somehow her father was there and he had been very rude. Then the noise the hyena made was so loud she woke and for a moment she did not know where she was and she was very afraid. Then she took the flashlight and shone it on the other cot that they had carried in after Harry had gone to sleep. She could see his bulk under the mosquito bar but somehow he had gotten his leg out and it hung down alongside the cot. The dressings had all come down and she could not look at it.

'Molo,' she called. 'Molo! Molo!'

Then she said, 'Harry, Harry!' Then her voice rising, 'Harry! Please. Oh Harry!'

There was no answer and she could not hear him breathing.

Outside the tent the hyena made the same strange noise that had awakened her. But she did not hear him for the beating of her heart.

Up in Michigan

Jim Gilmore came to Hortons Bay from Canada. He bought the blacksmith shop from old man Horton. Jim was short and dark with big moustaches and big hands. He was a good horseshoer and did not look much like a blacksmith even with his leather apron on. He lived upstairs above the blacksmith shop and took his meals at D. J. Smith's.

Liz Coates worked for Smith's. Mrs Smith, who was a very large clean woman, said Liz Coates was the neatest girl she'd ever seen. Liz had good legs and always wore clean gingham aprons and Jim noticed that her hair was always neat behind. He liked her face because it was so jolly but he never thought about her.

Liz liked Jim very much. She liked it the way he walked over from the shop and often went to the kitchen door to watch for him to start down the road. She liked it about his moustache. She liked it about how white his teeth were when he smiled. She liked it very much that he didn't look like a blacksmith. She liked it how much D. J. Smith and Mrs Smith liked Jim. One day she found that she liked it the way the hair was black on his arms and how white they were above the tanned line when he washed up in the washbasin outside the house. Liking that made her feel funny.

Hortons Bay, the town, was only five houses on the main road between Boyne City and Charlevoix. There was the general store and the post-office with a high false front and maybe a wagon hitched out in front, Smith's house, Stroud's house, Dilworth's house, Horton's house, Horton's house, and Van Hoosen's house. The houses were in a big grove of elm trees and the road was very sandy. Up the road a ways was the Methodist church and down the road the other direction was the township school. The blacksmith shop was painted red and faced the school.

A steep sandy road ran down the hill to the bay through the timber. From Smith's back door you could look out across the woods that ran down to the lake and across the bay. It was very beautiful in the spring and summer, the bay blue and bright and usually whitecaps on the lake out beyond the point from the breeze blowing from Charlevoix and Lake Michigan. From Smith's back door Liz could see ore barges way out in the lake going toward Boyne City. When she looked at them they didn't seem to be moving at all but if she went in and dried some more dishes and then came out again they would be out of sight beyond the point.

All the time now Liz was thinking about Jim Gilmore. He didn't seem to notice her much. He talked about the shop to D. J. Smith and about the Republican Party and James G. Blaine. In the evenings he read *The Toledo Blade* and the Grand Rapids paper by the lamp in the front room or went out spearing fish in the bay with a jacklight from D. J. Smith. In the fall he and Smith and Charley Wyman took a wagon and tent, grub, axes, their rifles, and two dogs and went on a trip to the pine plains beyond Vanderbilt deer hunting. Liz and Mrs Smith were cooking for four days for them before they started. Liz wanted to make something special for Jim to take but she didn't finally because she was afraid to ask Mrs Smith for the eggs and flour and afraid if she bought them Mrs Smith would catch her cooking. It would have been all right with Mrs Smith but Liz was afraid.

All the time Jim was gone on the deer-hunting trip Liz thought about him. It was awful while he was gone. She couldn't sleep well from thinking about him but she discovered it was fun to think about him too. If she let herself to it was better. The night before they were due to come back she didn't sleep at all, that is she didn't think she slept because it was all mixed up in a dream about not sleeping and really not sleeping. When she saw the wagon coming down the road she felt weak and sick sort of inside. She couldn't wait till she saw Jim and it seemed as though everything would be all right when he came. The wagon stopped outside under the elm and Mrs Smith and Liz went out. All the men had beards and there were three deer in the back of the wagon, their thin legs sticking stiff over the edge of the wagon box. Mrs Smith kissed D. J. and he hugged her. Jim said 'Hello, Liz,' and grinned. Liz hadn't known just what would happen when Jim got back but she was sure it would be something. Nothing had happened. The men were just home, that was all. Jim pulled the burlap sacks off the deer and Liz looked at them. One was a big buck. It was stiff and hard to lift out of the wagon.

'Did you shoot it, Jim?' Liz asked.

'Yeah. Ain't it a beauty?' Jim got it on to his back to carry into the smokehouse.

That night Charley Wyman stayed to supper at Smith's. It was too late to get back to Charlevoix. The men washed up and waited in the front room for supper.

'Ain't there something left in that crock, Jimmy?' D. J. Smith asked, and Jim went out to the wagon in the barn and fetched in the jug of whisky the men had taken hunting with them. It was a four-gallon jug and there was quite a little slopped back and forth in the bottom. Jim took a long pull on his way back to the house. It was hard to lift such a big jug up to drink out of it. Some of the whisky ran down on his shirtfront. The two men smiled when Jim came in with the jug. D. J. Smith sent for glasses and Liz brought them. D. J. poured out three big shots.

'Well, here's looking at you, D. J.,' said Charley Wyman.

'That damn big buck, Jimmy,' said D. J.

'Here's all the ones we missed, D. J.,' said Jim, and downed his liquor.

'Tastes good to a man.'

'Nothing like it at this time of year for what ails you.'

'How about another, boys?'

'Here's how, D. J.'

'Down the creek, boys.'

'Here's to next year.'

Jim began to feel great. He loved the taste and the feel of

whisky. He was glad to be back to a comfortable bed and warm food and the shop. He had another drink. The men came in to supper feeling hilarious but acting very respectable. Liz sat at the table after she put on the food and ate with the family. It was a good dinner. The men ate seriously. After supper they went into the front room again and Liz cleaned off with Mrs Smith. Then Mrs Smith went upstairs and pretty soon Smith came out and went upstairs too. Jim and Charley were still in the front room. Liz was sitting in the kitchen next to the stove pretending to read a book and thinking about Jim. She didn't want to go to bed yet because she knew Jim would be coming out and she wanted to see him as he went out so she could take the way he looked up to bed with her.

She was thinking about him hard and then Jim came out. His eyes were shining and his hair was a little rumpled. Liz looked down at her book. Jim came over back of her chair and stood there and she could feel him breathing and then he put his arms around her. Her breasts felt plump and firm and the nipples were erect under his hands. Liz was terribly frightened, no one had ever touched her, but she thought, 'He's come to me finally. He's really come.'

She held herself stiff because she was so frightened and did not know anything else to do and then Jim held her tight against the chair and kissed her. It was such a sharp, aching, hurting feeling that she thought she couldn't stand it. She felt Jim right through the back of the chair and she couldn't stand it and then something clicked inside of her and the feeling was warmer and softer. Jim held her tight hard against the chair and she wanted it now and Jim whispered, 'Come on for a walk.'

Liz took her coat off the peg on the kitchen wall and they went out the door. Jim had his arm around her and every little way they stopped and pressed against each other and Jim kissed her. There was no moon and they walked ankle-deep in the sandy road through the trees down to the dock and the warehouse on the bay. The water was lapping in the piles and the point was dark across the bay. It was cold but Liz was hot all over from being with Jim. They sat down in the shelter of the warehouse and Jim pulled Liz close to him. She was frightened. One of Jim's hands went inside her dress and stroked over her breast and the other hand was in her lap. She was very frightened and didn't know how he was going to go about things but she snuggled close to him. Then the hand that felt so big in her lap went away and was on her leg and started to move up it.

'Don't, Jim,' Liz said. Jim slid the hand farther up.

'You mustn't.' Neither Jim nor Jim's big hand paid any attention to her.

The boards were hard. Jim had her dress up and was trying to do something to her. She was frightened but she wanted it. She had to have it but it frightened her.

'You mustn't do it, Jim. You mustn't.'

'I got to. I'm going to. You know we got to.'

'No, we haven't, Jim. We ain't got to. Oh, it isn't right. Oh, it's so big and it hurts so. You can't. Oh, Jim. Jim. Oh.'

The hemlock planks of the docks were hard and splintery and cold and Jim was heavy on her and he had hurt her. Liz pushed him, she was so uncomfortable and cramped. Jim was asleep. He wouldn't move. She worked out from under him and sat up and straightened her skirt and coat and tried to do something with her hair. Jim was sleeping with his mouth a little open. Liz leaned over and kissed him on the cheek. He was still asleep. She lifted his head a little and shook it. He rolled his head over and swallowed. Liz started to cry. She walked over to the edge of the dock and looked down to the water. She was cold and miserable and everything felt gone. She walked back to where Jim was lying and shook him once to make sure. She was crying.

'Jim,' she said. 'Jim. Please, Jim.'

Jim stirred and curled a little tighter. Liz took off her coat and leaned over and covered him with it. She tucked it around him neatly and carefully. Then she walked across the dock and up the steep sandy road to go to bed. A cold mist was coming up through the woods from the bay.

On the Quai at Smyrna

The strange thing was, he said, how they screamed every night at midnight. I do not know why they screamed at that time. We were in the harbour and they were all on the pier and at midnight they started screaming. We used to turn the searchlight on them to quiet them. That always did the trick. We'd run the searchlight up and down over them two or three times and they stopped it. One time I was senior officer on the pier and a Turkish officer came up to me in a frightful rage because one of our sailors had been most insulting to him. So I told him the fellow would be sent on ship and be most severely punished. I asked him to point him out. So he pointed out a gunner's mate, most inoffensive chap. Said he'd been most frightfully and repeatedly insulting; talking to me through an interpreter. I couldn't imagine how the gunner's mate knew enough Turkish to be insulting. I called him over and said, 'And just in case you should have spoken to any Turkish officers.'

'I haven't spoken to any of them, sir.'

'I'm quite certain of it,' I said, 'but you'd best go on board ship and not come ashore again for the rest of the day.'

Then I told the Turk the man was being sent on board ship and would be most severely dealt with. Oh, most rigorously. He felt topping about it. Great friends we were.

The worst, he said, were the women with dead babies. You couldn't get the women to give up their dead babies. They'd have babies dead for six days. Wouldn't give them up. Nothing you could do about it. Had to take them away finally. Then

30

there was an old lady, most extraordinary case. I told it to a doctor and he said I was lying. We were clearing them off the pier, had to clear off the dead ones, and this old woman was lying on a sort of litter. They said, 'Will you have a look at her, sir?' So I had a look at her and just then she died and went absolutely stiff. Her legs drew up and she drew up from the waist and went quite rigid. Exactly as though she had been dead over night. She was quite dead and absolutely rigid. I told a medical chap about it and he told me it was impossible.

They were all out there on the pier and it wasn't at all like an earthquake or that sort of thing because they never knew about the Turk. They never knew what the old Turk would do. You remember when they ordered us not to come in to take off any more? I had the wind up when we came in that morning. He had any amount of batteries and could have blown us clean out of the water. We were going to come in, run close along the pier, let go the front and rear anchors, and then shell the Turkish quarter of the town. They would have blown us out of water but we would have blown the town simply to hell. They just fired a few blank charges at us as we came in. Kemal came down and sacked the Turkish commander. For exceeding his authority or some such thing. He got a bit above himself. It would have been the hell of a mess.

You remember the harbour. There were plenty of nice things floating around in it. That was the only time in my life I got so I dreamed about things. You didn't mind the women who were having babies as you did those with the dead ones. They had them all right. Surprising how few of them died. You just covered them over with something and let them go to it. They'd always pick out the darkest places in the hold to have them. None of them minded anything once they got off the pier.

The Greeks were nice chaps too. When they evacuated they had all their baggage animals they couldn't take off with them so they just broke their forelegs and dumped them into the shallow water. All those mules with their forelegs broken pushed over into the shallow water. It was all a pleasant business. My word, yes, a most pleasant business.

31

Indian Camp

Everybody was drunk. The whole battery was drunk going along the road in the dark. We were going to Champagne. The lieutenant kept riding his horse out into the fields and saying to him, 'I'm drunk, I tell you, mon vieux. Oh, I am so soused.' We went along the road all night in the dark and the adjutant kept riding up alongside my kitchen and saying, 'You must put it out. It is dangerous. It will be observed.' We were fifty kilometres from the front but this adjutant worried about the fire in my kitchen. It was funny going along that road. That was when I was a kitchen corporal.

At the lake shore there was another rowboat drawn up. The two Indians stood waiting.

Nick and his father got in the stern of the boat and the Indians shoved it off and one of them got in to row. Uncle George sat in the stern of the camp rowboat. The young Indian shoved the camp boat off and got in to row Uncle George.

The two boats started off in the dark. Nick heard the oar-locks of the other boat quite a way ahead of them in the mist. The Indians rowed with quick choppy strokes. Nick lay back with his father's arm around him. It was cold on the water. The Indian who was rowing them was working very hard, but the other boat moved farther ahead in the mist all the time.

'Where are we going, Dad?' Nick, asked.

'Over to the Indian Camp. There is an Indian lady very sick.'

'Oh,' said Nick.

Across the bay they found the other boat beached. Uncle George was smoking a cigar in the dark. The young Indian pulled the boat way up on the beach. Uncle George gave both the Indians cigars.

They walked up from the beach through a meadow that was soaking wet with dew, following the young Indian who carried a lantern. Then they went into the woods and followed a trail that led to the logging road that ran back into the hills. It was much lighter on the logging road as the timber was cut away on both sides. The young Indian stopped and blew out his lantern and they all walked on along the road.

They came around a bend and a dog came out barking. Ahead were the lights of the shanties where the Indian bark-peelers lived. More dogs rushed out at them. The two Indians sent them back to the shanties. In the shanty nearest the road there was a light in the window. An old woman stood in the doorway holding a lamp.

Inside on a wooden bunk lay a young Indian woman. She had been trying to have her baby for two days. All the old women in the camp had been helping her. The men had moved off up the road to sit in the dark and smoke out of range of the noise she made. She screamed just as Nick and the two Indians followed his father and Uncle George into the shanty. She lay in the lower bunk, very big under a quilt. Her head was turned to one side. In the upper bunk was her husband. He had cut his foot very badly with an axe three days before. He was smoking a pipe. The room smelled very bad.

Nick's father ordered some water to be put on the stove, and while it was heating he spoke to Nick.

'This lady is going to have a baby, Nick,' he said.

'I know,' said Nick.

'You don't know,' said his father. 'Listen to me. What she is going through is called being in labour. The baby wants to be born and she wants it to be born. All her muscles are trying to get the baby born. That is what is happening when she screams.'

'I see,' Nick said.

Just then the woman cried out.

'Oh, Daddy, can't you give her something to make her stop screaming?' asked Nick.

'No. I haven't any anaesthetic,' his father said. 'But her screams are not important. I don't hear them because they are not important.'

The husband in the upper bunk rolled over against the wall.

The woman in the kitchen motioned to the doctor that the water was hot. Nick's father went into the kitchen and poured about half the water out of the big kettle into a basin. Into the water left in the kettle he put several things he unwrapped from a handkerchief.

'Those must boil,' he said, and began to scrub his hands in the basin of hot water with a cake of soap he had brought from the camp. Nick watched his father's hands scrubbing each other with the soap. While his father washed his hands very carefully and thoroughly, he talked.

'You see, Nick, babies are supposed to be born head first, but sometimes they're not. When they're not they make a lot of trouble for everybody. Maybe I'll have to operate on this lady. We'll know in a little while.'

When he was satisfied with his hands he went in and went to work.

'Pull back that quilt, will you, George?' he said. 'I'd rather not touch it.'

Later when he started to operate Uncle George and three Indian men held the woman still. She bit Uncle George on the arm and Uncle George said, 'Damn squaw bitch!' and the young Indian who had rowed Uncle George over laughed at him. Nick held the basin for his father. It all took a long time.

His father picked the baby up and slapped it to make it breathe and handed it to the old woman.

'See, it's a boy, Nick,' he said. 'How do you like being an interne?'

Nick said, 'All right.' He was looking away so as not to see what his father was doing.

'There. That gets it,' said his father and put something into the basin.

Nick didn't look at it.

'Now,' his father said, 'there's some stitches to put in. You can watch this or not, Nick, just as you like. I'm going to sew up the incision I made.'

Nick did not watch. His curiosity had been gone for a long time.

His father finished and stood up. Uncle George and the three Indian men stood up. Nick put the basin out in the kitchen.

Uncle George looked at his arm. The young Indian smiled reminiscently.

'I'll put some peroxide on that, George,' the doctor said.

He bent over the Indian woman. She was quiet now and her eyes were closed. She looked very pale. She did not know what had become of the baby or anything.

'I'll be back in the morning,' the doctor said, standing up. 'The nurse should be here from St Ignace by noon and she'll bring everything we need.'

He was feeling exalted and talkative as football players are in the dressing-room after a game.

'That's one for the medical journal, George,' he said. 'Doing a Caesarian with a jack-knife and sewing it up with nine-foot, tapered gut leaders.'

Uncle George was standing against the wall, looking at his arm.

'Oh, you're a great man, all right,' he said.

'Ought to have a look at the proud father. They're usually the worst sufferers in these little affairs,' the doctor said. 'I must say he took it all pretty quietly.'

He pulled back the blanket from the Indian's head. His hand came away wet. He mounted the edge of the lower bunk with the lamp in one hand and looked in. The Indian lay with his face toward the flower. His throat had been cut from ear to ear. The blood had flowed down into a pool where his body sagged the bunk. His head rested on his left arm. The open razor lay, edge up, in the blankets.

'Take Nick out of the shanty, George,' the doctor said.

There was no need of that. Nick, standing in the door of the kitchen, had a good view of the upper bunk when his father, the lamp in one hand, tipped the Indian's head back.

It was beginning to be daylight when they walked along the logging road back toward the lake.

'I'm terribly sorry I brought you along, Nickie,' said his

35

father, all his post-operative exhilaration gone. 'It was an awful mess to put you through.'

'Do ladies always have such a hard time having babies?' Nick asked.

'No, that was very, very exceptional.'

'Why did he kill himself, Daddy?'

'I don't know, Nick. He couldn't stand things, I guess.'

'Do many men kill themselves, Daddy?'

'Not very many, Nick.'

'Do many women?'

'Hardly ever.'

'Don't they ever?'

'Oh, yes. They do sometimes.'

'Daddy?'

'Yes.'

'Where did Uncle George go?'

'He'll turn up all right.'

'Is dying hard, Daddy?'

'No, I think it's pretty easy, Nick. It all depends.'

They were seated in the boat, Nick at the stern, his father rowing. The sun was coming up over the hills. A bass jumped, making a circle in the water. Nick trailed his hand in the water. It felt warm in the sharp chill of the morning.

In the early morning on the lake sitting in the stern of the boat with his father rowing, he felt quite sure that he would never die.

The Doctor and the Doctor's Wife

Minarets stuck up in the rain out of Adranople across the mud flats. The carts were jammed for thirty miles along the Karagatch road. Water buffalo and cattle were hauling carts through the mud. No end and no beginning. Just carts loaded with everything they owned. The old men and women, soaked through, walked along keeping the cattle moving. The Maritza was running yellow almost up to the bridge. Carts were jammed solid on the bridge with camels bobbing along through them. Green cavalry herded along the procession. Women and kids were in the carts couched with mattresses, mirrors, sewing-machines, bundles. There was a woman having a kid with a young girl holding a blanket over her and crying. Scared sick looking at it. It rained all through the evacuation.

Dick Boulton came from the Indian camp to cut up logs for Nick's father. He brought his son Eddy and another Indian named Billy Tabeshaw with him. They came in through the back gate out of the woods, Eddy carrying the long cross-cut saw. It flopped over his shoulder and made a musical sound as he walked. Billy Tabeshaw carried two big cant-hooks. Dick had three axes under his arm.

He turned and shut the gate. The others went on ahead of him down to the lake shore where the logs were buried in the sand.

The logs had been lost from the big lob booms that were towed down the lake to the mill by the steamer *Magic*.

They had drifted up on to the beach and if nothing were done about them sooner or later the crew of the *Magic* would come along the shore in a row-boat, spot the logs, drive an iron spike with a ring on it into the end of each one and then tow them out into the lake to make a new boom. But the lumbermen might never come for them because a few logs were not worth the price of a crew to gather them. If no one came for them they would be left to waterlog and rot on the beach.

Nick's father always assumed that this was what would happen, and hired the Indians to come down from the camp and cut the logs up with the cross-cut saw and split them with a wedge to make cord wood and chunks for the open fireplace. Dick Boulton walked around past the cottage down to the lake. There were four big beech logs lying almost buried in the sand. Eddy hung the saw up by one of its handles in the crotch of a tree. Dick put the three axes down on the little dock. Dick was a half-breed and many of the farmers around the lake believed he was really a white man. He was very lazy but a great worker once he was started. He took a plug of tobacco out of his pocket, bit off a chew, and spoke in Ojibway to Eddy and Billy Tabeshaw.

They sunk the ends of their cant-hooks into one of the logs and swung against it to loosen it in the sand. They swung their weight against the shafts of the cant-hooks. The log moved in the sand. Dick Boulton turned to Nick's father.

'Well, Doc,' he said, 'that's a nice lot of lumber you've stolen.'

'Don't talk that way, Dick,' the doctor said. 'It's driftwood.'

Eddy and Billy Tabeshaw had rocked the log out of the wet sand and rolled it toward the water.

'Put it right in,' Dick Boulton shouted.

'What are you doing that for?' asked the doctor.

'Wash it off. Clean off the sand on account of the saw. I want to see who it belongs to,' Dick said.

The log was just awash in the lake. Eddy and Billy Tabeshaw leaned on their cant-hooks sweating in the sun. Dick kneeled down in the sand and looked at the mark of the scaler's hammer in the wood at the end of the log.

'It belongs to White and McNally,' he said, standing up and brushing off his trouser knees.

The doctor was very uncomfortable.

'You'd better not saw it up then, Dick,' he said, shortly.

'Don't get huffy, Doc,' said Dick. 'Don't get huffy. I don't care who you steal from. It's none of my business.'

'If you think the logs are stolen, leave them alone and take your tools back to the camp,' the doctor said. His face was red.

'Don't go off at half cock, Doc,' Dick said. He spat tobacco juice on the log. It slid off, thinning in the water. 'You know they're stolen as well as I do. It don't make any difference to me.'

'All right. If you think the logs are stolen, take your stuff and get out.'

'Now, Doc—'

'Take your stuff and get out.'

'Listen, Doc.'

'If you call me Doc once again, I'll knock your eye teeth down your throat.'

'Oh, no, you won't, Doc.'

Dick Boulton looked at the doctor. Dick was a big man. He knew how big a man he was. He liked to get into fights. He was happy. Eddy and Billy Tabeshaw leaned on their cant-hooks and looked at the doctor. The doctor chewed the beard on his lower lip and looked at Dick Boulton. Then he turned away and walked up the hill to the cottage. They could see from his back how angry he was. They all watched him walk up the hill and go inside the cottage.

Dick said something in Ojibway. Eddy laughed but Billy Tabeshaw looked very serious. He did not understand English but he had sweat all the time the row was going on. He was fat with only a few hairs of moustache like a Chinaman. He picked up the two cant-hooks. Dick picked up the axes and Eddy took the saw down from the tree. They started off and walked up past the cottage and out the back gate into the woods. Dick left the gate open. Billy Tabeshaw went back and fastened it. They were gone through the woods.

In the cottage the doctor, sitting on the bed in his room, saw a pile of medical journals on the floor by the bureau. They were still in their wrappers unopened. It irritated him.

'Aren't you going back to work, dear?' asked the doctor's wife from the room where she was lying with the blinds drawn.

'No!'

'Was anything the matter?'

'I had a row with Dick Boulton.'

'Oh,' said his wife. 'I hope you didn't lose your temper, Henry.'

'No,' said the doctor.

'Remember, that he who ruleth his spirit is greater than he that taketh a city,' said his wife. She was a Christian Scientist. Her Bible, her copy of *Science and Health*, and her *Quarterly* were on a table beside her bed in the darkened room.

Her husband did not answer. He was sitting on his bed now, cleaning a shotgun. He pushed the magazine full of heavy yellow shells and pumped them out again. They were scattered on the bed.

'Henry,' his wife called. Then paused a moment. 'Henry!'

'Yes,' the doctor said.

'You didn't say anything to Boulton to anger him, did you?'

'No,' said the doctor.

'What was the trouble about, dear?'

'Nothing much.'

'Tell me, Henry. Please don't try and keep anything from me. What was the trouble about?'

'Well, Dick owes me a lot of money for pulling his squaw through pneumonia and I guess he wanted a row so he wouldn't have to take it out in work.'

His wife was silent. The doctor wiped his gun carefully with a rag. He pushed the shells back in against the spring of the magazine. He sat with the gun on his knees. He was very fond of it. Then he heard his wife's voice from the darkened room.

'Dear, I don't think, I really don't think that anyone would really do a thing like that.'

'No?' the doctor said.

'No. I can't really believe that anyone would do a thing of that sort intentionally.'

The doctor stood up and put the shotgun in the corner behind the dresser.

'Are you going out, dear?' his wife said.

'I think I'll go for a walk,' the doctor said.

'If you see Nick, dear, will you tell him his mother wants to see him?' his wife said.

The doctor went out on the porch. The screen door slammed behind him. He heard his wife catch her breath when the door slammed.

'Sorry,' he said, outside her window with the blinds drawn.

'It's all right, dear,' she said.

He walked in the heat out of the gate and along the path into the hemlock woods. It was cool in the woods even on such a hot day. He found Nick sitting with his back against a tree, reading.

'Your mother wants you to come and see her,' the doctor said.

'I want to go with you,' Nick said.

His father looked down at him.

'All right. Come on, then,' his father said. 'Give me the book, I'll put it in my pocket.'

'I know where there's black squirrels, Daddy,' Nick said.

'All right,' said his father. 'Let's go there.'

The End of Something

We were in a garden at Mons. Young Buckley came in with his patrol from across the river. The first German I saw climbed up over the garden wall. We waited till he got one leg over and then potted him. He had so much equipment on and looked awfully surprised and fell down into the garden. Then three more came over farther down the wall. We shot them. They all came just like that.

In the old days Hortons Bay was a lumbering town. No one who lived in it was out of sound of the big saws in the mill by the lake. Then one year there were no more logs to make lumber. The lumber schooners came into the bay and were loaded with the cut of the mill that stood stacked in the yard. All the piles of lumber were carried away. The big mill building had all its machinery that was removable taken out and hoisted on board one of the schooners by the men who had worked in the mill. The schooner moved out of the bay toward the open lake carrying the two great saws, the travelling carriage that hurled the logs against the revolving, circular saws, and all the rollers, wheels, belts, and iron piled on a hull-deep load of lumber. Its open hold covered with canvas and lashed tight, the sails of the schooner filled and it moved out into the open lake, carrying with it everything that had made the mill a mill and Hortons Bay a town.

The one-storey bunk houses, the eating-house, the company store, the mill offices, and the big mill itself stood deserted in the acres of sawdust that covered the swampy meadow by the shore of the bay.

Ten years later there was nothing of the mill left except the broken white limestone of its foundations showing through the swampy second growth as Nick and Marjorie rowed along the shore. They were trolling along the edge of the channel bank where the bottom dropped off suddenly from sandy shallows to twelve feet of dark water. They were trolling on their way to the point to set night lines for rainbow trout.

'There's our old ruin, Nick,' Marjorie said.

Nick, rowing, looked at the white stone in the green trees.

'There it is,' he said.

'Can you remember when it was a mill?' Marjorie asked.

'I can just remember,' Nick said.

'It seems more like a castle,' Marjorie said.

Nick said nothing. They rowed on out of sight of the mill, following the shore line. Then Nick cut across the bay.

'They aren't striking,' he said.

'No,' Marjorie said. She was intent on the rod all the time they trolled, even when she talked. She loved to fish. She loved to fish with Nick.

Close beside the boat a big trout broke the surface of the water. Nick pulled hard on one oar so the boat would turn and the bait spinning far behind would pass where the trout was feeding. As the trout's back came up out of the water the minnows jumped wildly. They sprinkled the surface like a handful of shot thrown into the water. Another trout broke water, feeding on the other side of the boat.

'They're feeding,' Marjorie said.

'But they won't strike,' Nick said.

He rowed the boat around to troll past both the feeding fish, then headed it for the point. Marjorie did not reel in until the boat touched the shore.

They pulled the boat up the beach and Nick lifted out a pail of live perch. The perch swam in the water in the pail. Nick caught three of them with his hands and cut their heads off and skinned them while Marjorie chased her hands in the bucket, finally caught a perch, cut its head off, and skinned it. Nick looked at her fish.

43

'You don't want to take the ventral fin out,' he said. 'It'll be all right for bait but it's better with the ventral fin in.'

He hooked each of the skinned perch through the tail. There were two hooks attached to a leader on each rod. Then Marjorie rowed the boat out over the channel-bank, holding the line in her teeth, and looking toward Nick, who stood on the shore holding the rod and letting the line run out from the reel.

'That's about right,' he called.

'Should I let it drop?' Marjorie called back, holding the line in her hand.

'Sure. Let it go.' Marjorie dropped the line overboard and watched the baits go down through the water.

She came in with the boat and ran the second line out the same way. Each time Nick set a heavy slab of driftwood across the butt of the rod to hold it solid and propped it up at an angle with a small slab. He reeled in the slack line so the line ran taut out to where the bait rested on the sandy floor of the channel and set the click on the reel. When a trout, feeding on the bottom, took the bait it would run with it, taking line out of the reel in a rush and making the reel sing with the click on. Marjorie rowed up the point a little way so she would not disturb the line. She pulled hard on the oars and the boat went up the beach. Little waves came in with it. Marjorie stepped out of the boat and Nick pulled the boat high up the beach.

'What's the matter, Nick?' Marjorie asked.

'I don't know,' Nick said, getting wood for the fire.

They made a fire with driftwood. Marjorie went to the boat and brought a blanket. The evening breeze blew the smoke toward the point, so Marjorie spread the blanket out between the fire and the lake.

Marjorie sat on the blanket with her back to the fire and waited for Nick. He came over and sat down beside her on the blanket. In back of them was the close second-growth timber of the point and in front was the bay with the mouth of Hortons Creek. It was not quite dark. The firelight went as far as the water. They could both see the two steel rods at an angle over the dark water. The fire glinted on the reels.

Marjorie unpacked the basket of supper.

'I don't feel like eating,' said Nick.

'Come on and eat, Nick.'

'All right.'

They ate without talking, and watched the two rods and the firelight in the water.

'There's going to be a moon tonight,' said Nick. He looked across the bay to the hills that were beginning to sharpen across the sky. Beyond the hills he knew the moon was coming up.

'I know it,' Marjorie said happily.

'You know everything,' Nick said.

'Oh, Nick, please cut it out! Please, please don't be that way!'

'I can't help it,' Nick said. 'You do. You know everything. That's the trouble. You know you do.'

Marjorie did not say anything.

'I've taught you everything. You know you do. What don't you know, anyway?'

'Oh, shut up,' Marjorie said. 'There comes the moon.'

They sat on the blanket without touching each other and watched the moon rise.

'You don't have to talk silly,' Marjorie said. 'What's really the matter?'

'I don't know.'

'Of course you know.'

'No, I don't.'

'Go on and say it.'

Nick looked on at the moon, coming up over the hills.

'It isn't fun any more.'

He was afraid to look at Marjorie. Then he looked at her. She sat there with her back toward him. He looked at her back. 'It isn't fun any more. Not any of it.'

She didn't say anything. He went on. 'I feel as though everything was gone to hell inside of me. I don't know, Marge. I don't know what to say.'

He looked on at her back.

'Isn't love any fun?' Marjorie said.

'No,' Nick said. Marjorie stood up. Nick sat there, his head in his hands.

'I'm going to take the boat,' Marjorie called to him. 'You can walk back around the point.'

'All right,' Nick said. 'I'll push the boat off for you.'

'You don't need to,' she said. She was afloat in the boat on the water with the moonlight on it. Nick went back and lay down with his face in the blanket by the fire. He could hear Marjorie rowing on the water.

He lay there for a long time. He lay there while he heard Bill come into the clearing walking around through the woods. He felt Bill coming up to the fire. Bill didn't touch him, either.

'Did she go all right?' Bill said.

'Yes,' Nick said, lying, his face on the blanket.

'Have a scene?'

'No, there wasn't any scene.'

'How do you feel?'

'Oh, go away, Bill! Go away for a while.'

Bill selected a sandwich from the lunch basket and walked over to have a look at the rods.

The Three-Day Blow

It was a frightfully hot day. We'd jammed an absolutely perfect barricade across the bridge. It was simply priceless. A big old wrought-iron grating from the front of a house. Too heavy to lift and you could shoot through it and they would have to climb over it. It was absolutely topping. They tried to get over it, and we potted them from forty yards. They rushed it, and officers came out alone and worked on it. It was an absolutely perfect obstacle. Their officers were very fine. We were frightfully put out when we heard the flank had gone, and we had to fall back.

The rain stopped as Nick turned into the road that went up through the orchard. The fruit had been picked and the fall wind blew through the bare trees. Nick stopped and picked up a Wagner apple from beside the road, shiny in the brown grass from the rain. He put the apple in the pocket of his Mackinaw coat.

The road came out of the orchard on to the top of the hill. There was the cottage, the porch bare, smoke coming from the chimney. In back was the garage, the chicken coop, and the second-growth timber like a hedge against the woods behind. The big trees swayed far over in the wind as he watched. It was the first of the autumn storms.

As Nick crossed the open field above the orchard the door of the cottage opened and Bill came out. He stood on the porch looking out.

'Well, Wemedge?' he said.

47

'Hey, Bill,' Nick said, coming up the steps.

They stood together, looking out across the country, down over the orchard, beyond the road, across the lower fields and the woods of the point to the lake. The wind was blowing straight down the lake. They could see the surf along Ten Mile point.

'She's blowing,' Nick said.

'She'll blow like that for three days,' Bill said.

'Is your dad in?' Nick said.

'No. He's out with the gun. Come on in.'

Nick went inside the cottage. There was a big fire in the fire place. The wind made it roar. Bill shut the door.

'Have a drink?' he said.

He went out to the kitchen and came back with two glasses and a pitcher of water. Nick reached the whiskey bottle from the shelf above the fireplace.

'All right?' he said.

'Good,' said Bill.

They sat in front of the fire and drank the Irish whiskey and water.

'It's got a swell, smoky taste,' Nick said, and looked at me fire through the glass.

'That's the peat,' Bill said.

'You can't get peat into liquor,' Nick said.

'That doesn't make any difference,' Bill said.

'You ever seen any peat?' Nick asked.

'No,' said Bill.

His shoes, stretched out on the hearth, began to steam in front of the fire.

'Better take your shoes off,' Bill said.

'I haven't got any socks on.'

'Take them off and dry them and I'll get you some,' Bill said. He went upstairs into the loft and Nick heard him walking about overhead. Upstairs was open under the roof and was where Bill and his father and he, Nick, sometimes slept. In the back was a dressing-room. They moved the cots back out of the rain and covered them with rubber blankets.

Bill came down with a pair of heavy wool socks.

'It's getting late to go around without socks,' he said.

'I hate to start them again,' Nick said. He pulled the socks on and slumped back in the chair, putting his feet up on the screen in front of the fire.

'You'll dent in the screen,' Bill said. Nick swung his feet over to the side of the fireplace.

'Got anything to read?' he asked.

'Only the paper.'

'What did the Cards do?'

'Dropped a double header to the Giants.'

'That ought to cinch it for them.'

'It's a gift,' Bill said. 'As long as McGraw can buy every good ball player in the league there's nothing to it.'

'He can't buy them all,' Nick said.

'He buys all the ones he wants,' Bill said. 'Or he makes them discontented so they have to trade them to him.'

'Like Heinie Zim,' Nick agreed.

'That bonehead will do him a lot of good.'

Bill stood up.

'He can hit,' Nick offered. The heat from the fire was baking his legs.

'He's a sweet fielder, too,' Bill said. 'But he loses ball games.'

'Maybe that's what McGraw wants him for,' Nick suggested.

'Maybe,' Bill said.

'There's more always to it than we know about,' Nick said.

'Of course. But we've got pretty good dope for being so far away.'

'Like how much better you can pick them if you don't see the horses.'

'That's it.'

Bill reached down the whiskey bottle. His big hand went all the way around it. He poured the whiskey into the glass Nick held out.

'How much water?'

'Just the same.'

He sat down on the floor beside Nick's chair.

'It's good when the fall storms come, isn't it?' Nick said.

'It's swell.'

'It's the best time of year,' Nick said.

'Wouldn't it be hell to be in town,' Bill said.

'I'd like to see the World Series,' Nick said.

'Well, they're always in New York or Philadelphia now,' Bill said. 'That doesn't do us any good.'

'I wonder if the Cards will ever win a pennant?'

'Not in our lifetime,' Bill said.

'Gee, they'd go crazy,' Nick said.

'Do you remember when they got going that once before they had the train wreck?'

'Boy!' Nick said, remembering.

Bill reached over to the table under the window for the book that lay there, face down, where he had put it when he went to the door. He held his glass in one hand and the book in the other, leaning back against Nick's chair.

'What are you reading?'

'*Richard Feverel.*'

'I couldn't get into it.'

'It's all right,' Bill said. 'It ain't a bad book, Wemedge.'

'What else have you got I haven't read?' Nick asked.

'Did you read *Fortitude*?'

'It's fine,' Nick said. 'That's a real book. That's where his old man is after him all the time. Have you got any more by Walpole?'

'*The Dark Front*,' Bill said. 'It's about Russia.'

'What does he know about Russia?' Nick asked.

'I don't know. You can't ever tell about those guys. Maybe he was there when he was a boy. He's got a lot of dope on it.'

'I'd like to meet him,' Nick said.

'I'd like to meet Chesterton,' Bill said.

'I wish he was here now,' Nick said. 'We'd take him fishing on the 'Voix tomorrow.'

'I wonder if he'd like to go fishing,' Bill said.

'Sure,' said Nick. 'He must be about the best guy there is. Do you remember *The Flying Inn*?'

'If an angel out of heaven
  Gives you something else to drink,
  Thank him for his kind intentions;
  Go and pour them down the sink!'

50

'That's right,' said Nick. 'I guess he's a better guy than Walpole.'

'Oh, he's a better guy all right,' Bill said.

'But Walpole's a better writer.'

'I don't know,' Nick said. 'Chesterton's a classic.'

'Walpole's a classic, too,' Bill insisted.

'I wish we had them both here,' Nick said. 'We'd take them both fishing to the 'Voix tomorrow.'

'Let's get drunk,' Bill said.

'All right,' Nick agreed.

'My old man won't care,' Bill said.

'Are you sure?' said Nick.

'I know it,' Bill said.

'I'm a little drunk now,' Nick said.

'You aren't drunk,' Bill said.

He got up from the floor and reached for the whiskey bottle. Nick held out his glass. His eyes fixed on it while Bill poured.

Bill poured the glass half full of whiskey.

'Put in your own water,' he said. 'There's just one more shot.'

'Got any more?' Nick asked.

'There's plenty more but dad only likes me to drink what's open.'

'Sure,' said Nick.

'He says opening bottles is what makes drunkards,' Bill explained.

'That's right,' said Nick. He was impressed. He had never thought of that before. He had always thought it was solitary drinking that made drunkards.

'How is your dad?' he asked respectfully.

'He's all right,' Bill said. 'He gets a little wild sometimes.'

'He's a swell guy,' Nick said. He poured water into his glass out of the pitcher. It mixed slowly with the whiskey. There was more whiskey than water.

'You bet your life he is,' Bill said.

'My old man's all right,' Nick said.

'You're damn right he is,' said Bill.

'He claims he's never taken a drink in his life,' Nick said, as though announcing a scientific fact.

'Well, he's a doctor. My old man's a painter. That's different.'

'He's missed a lot,' Nick said sadly.

'You can't tell,' Bill said. 'Everything's got its compensations.'

'He says he's missed a lot himself,' Nick confessed.

'Well, dad's had a tough time,' Bill said.

'It all evens up,' Nick said.

They sat looking into the fire and thinking of this profound truth.

'I'll get a chunk from the back porch,' Nick said. He had noticed while looking into the fire that the fire was dying down. Also he wished to show he could hold his liquor and be practical. Even if his father had never touched a drop Bill was not going to get him drunk before he himself was drunk.

'Bring one of the big beech chunks,' Bill said. He was also being consciously practical.

Nick came in with the log through the kitchen and in passing knocked a pan off the kitchen table. He laid the log down and picked up the pan. It contained dried apricots, soaking in water. He carefully picked up all the apricots off the floor, some of them had gone under the stove, and put them back in the pan. He dipped some more water on to them from the pail by the table. He felt proud of himself. He had been thoroughly practical.

He came in carrying the log and Bill got up from the chair and helped him put it on the fire.

'That's a swell log,' Nick said.

'I'd been saving it for the bad weather,' Bill said. 'A log like that will burn all night.'

'There'll be coals left to start the fire in the morning,' Nick said.

'That's right,' Bill agreed. They were conducting the conversation on a high plane.

'Let's have another drink,' Nick said.

'I think there's another bottle open in the locker,' Bill said.

He kneeled down in the corner in front of the locker and brought out a square-faced bottle.

'It's Scotch,' he said.

'I'll get some more water,' Nick said. He went out into the

52

kitchen again. He filled the pitcher with the dipper, dipping cold spring water from the pail. On his way back to the living-room he passed a mirror in the dining-room and looked in it. His face looked strange. He smiled at the face in the mirror and it grinned back at him. He winked at it and went on. It was not his face, but it didn't make any difference.

Bill poured out the drinks.

'That's an awfully big shot,' Nick said.

'Not for us, Wemedge,' Bill said.

'What'll we drink to?' Nick asked, holding up the glass.

'Let's drink to fishing,' Bill said.

'All right,' Nick said. 'Gentlemen, I give you fishing.'

'All fishing,' Bill said. 'Everywhere.'

'Fishing,' Nick said. 'That's what we drink to.'

'It's better than baseball,' Bill said.

'There isn't any comparison,' said Nick. 'How did we ever get talking about baseball?'

'It was a mistake,' Bill said. 'Baseball is a game for louts.'

They drank all that was in their glasses.

'Now let's drink to Chesterton.'

'And Walpole,' Nick interposed.

Nick poured out the liquor. Bill poured in the water. They looked at each other. They felt very fine.

'Gentlemen,' Bill said, 'I give you Chesterton and Walpole.'

'Exactly, gentlemen,' Nick said.

They drank. Bill filled up the glasses. They sat down in the big chairs in front of the fire.

'You were very wise, Wemedge,' Bill said.

'What do you mean?' asked Nick.

'To bust off that Marge business,' Bill said.

'I guess so,' said Nick.

'It was the only thing to do. If you hadn't, by now you'd be back home working trying to get money enough to get married.'

Nick said nothing.

'Once a man's married he's absolutely bitched,' Bill went on. 'He hasn't got anything more. Nothing. Not a damn thing. He's done for. You've seen the guys that get married.'

Nick said nothing.

'You can tell them,' Bill said. 'They get this sort of fat married look. They're done for.'

'Sure,' said Nick.

'It was probably bad busting it off,' Bill said. 'But you always fall for somebody else and then it's all right. Fall for them but don't let them ruin you.'

'Yes,' said Nick.

'If you'd have married her you would have had to marry the whole family. Remember her mother and that guy she married.'

Nick nodded.

'Imagine having them around the house all the time and going to Sunday dinners at their house, and having them over to dinner and her telling Marge all the time what to do and how to act.'

Nick sat quiet.

'You came out of it damned well,' Bill said. 'Now she can marry somebody of her own sort and settle down and be happy. You can't mix oil and water and you can't mix that sort of thing any more than if I'd marry Ida that works for Strattons. She'd probably like it, too.'

Nick said nothing. The liquor had all died out of him and left him alone. Bill wasn't there. He wasn't sitting in front of the fire or going fishing tomorrow with Bill and his dad or anything. He wasn't drunk. It was all gone. All he knew was that he had once had Marjorie and that he had lost her. She was gone and he had sent her away. That was all that mattered. He might never see her again. Probably he never would. It was all gone, finished.

'Let's have another drink,' Nick said.

Bill poured it out. Nick splashed in a little water.

'If you'd gone on that way we wouldn't be here now,' Bill said.

That was true. His original plan had been to go down home and get a job. Then he had planned to stay in Charlevoix all winter so he could be near Marge. Now he did not know what he was going to do.

'Probably we wouldn't even be going fishing tomorrow,' Bill said. 'You had the right dope, all right.'

'I couldn't help it,' Nick said.

'I know. That's the way it works out,' Bill said.

'All of a sudden everything was over,' Nick said. 'I don't know why it was. I couldn't help it. Just like when the three-day blows come now and rip all the leaves off the trees.'

'Well, it's over. That's the point,' Bill said.

'It was my fault,' Nick said.

'It doesn't make any difference whose fault it was,' Bill said.

'No, I suppose not,' Nick said.

The big thing was that Marjorie was gone and that probably he would never see her again. He had talked to her about how they would go to Italy together and the fun they would have. Places they would be together. It was all gone now.

'So long as it's over that's all that matters,' Bill said. 'I tell you, Wemedge, I was worried while it was going on. You played it right. I understand her mother is sore as hell. She told a lot of people you were engaged.'

'We weren't engaged,' Nick said.

'It was all around that you were.'

'I can't help it,' Nick said. 'We weren't.'

'Weren't you going to get married?' Bill asked.

'Yes. But we weren't engaged,' Nick said.

'What's the difference?' Bill said judicially.

'I don't know. There's a difference.'

'I don't see it,' said Bill.

'All right,' said Nick. 'Let's get drunk.'

'All right,' Bill said. 'Let's get really drunk.'

'Let's get drunk and then go swimming,' Nick said.

He drank off his glass.

'I'm sorry as hell about her but what could I do?' he said. 'You know what her mother was like!'

'She was terrible,' Bill said.

'All of a sudden it was over,' Nick said. 'I oughtn't to talk about it.'

'You aren't,' Bill said. 'I talked about it and now I'm through. We won't ever speak about it again. You don't want to think about it. You might get back into it again.'

Nick had not thought about that. It had seemed so absolute. That was a thought. That made him feel better.

'Sure,' he said. 'There's always that danger.'

He felt happy now. There was not anything that was irrevocable. He might go into town Saturday night. Tomorrow was Thursday.

'There's always a chance,' he said.

'You'll have to watch yourself,' Bill said.

'I'll watch myself,' he said.

He felt happy. Nothing was finished. Nothing was ever lost. He would go into town on Saturday. He felt lighter, as he had felt before Bill started to talk about it. There was always a way out.

'Let's take the guns and go down to the point and look for your dad,' Nick said.

'All right.'

Bill took down the two shotguns from the rack on the wall. He opened a box of shells. Nick put on his Mackinshaw coat and his shoes. His shoes were stiff from drying. He was still quite drunk but his head was clear.

'How do you feel?' Nick asked.

'Swell. I've just got a good edge on,' Bill was buttoning up his sweater.

'There's no use getting drunk.'

'No. We ought to get outdoors.'

They stepped out the door. The wind was blowing a gale.

'The birds will lie right down in the grass with this,' Nick said.

They struck down toward the orchard.

'I saw a woodcock this morning,' Bill said.

'Maybe we'll jump him,' Nick said.

'You can't shoot in this wind,' Bill said.

Outside now the Marge business was no longer so tragic. It was not even very important. The wind blew everything like that away.

'It's coming right off the big lake,' Nick said.

Against the wind they heard the thud of a shotgun.

'That's dad,' Bill said. 'He's down in the swamp.'

'Let's cut down that way,' Nick said.

'Let's cut across the lower meadow and see if we jump anything,' Bill said.

56

'All right,' Nick said.

None of it was important now. The wind blew it out of his head. Still he could always go into town Saturday night. It was a good thing to have in reserve.

The Battler

They shot the six cabinet ministers at half past six in the morning against the wall of a hospital. There were pools of water in the courtyard. There were wet dead leaves on the paving of the court-yard. It rained hard. All the shutters of the hospital were nailed shut. One of the ministers was sick with typhoid. Two soldiers carried him downstairs and out into the rain. They tried to hold him up against the wall but he sat down in a puddle of water. The other five stood very quietly against the wall. Finally the officer told the soldiers it was no good trying to make him stand up. When they fired the first volley he was sitting down in the water with his head on his knees.

Nick stood up. He was all right. He looked up the track at the lights of the caboose going out of sight around the curve. There was water on both sides of the track, then tamarack swamp.

He felt his knee. The pants were torn and the skin was barked. His hands were scraped and there were sand and cinders driven up under his nails. He went over to the edge of the track down the little slope to the water and washed his hands. He washed them carefully in the cold water, getting the dirt out from the nails. He squatted down and bathed his knee.

That lousy crut of a brakeman. He would get him some day. He would know him again. That was a fine way to act.

'Come here, kid,' he said. 'I got something for you.'

He had fallen for it. What a lousy kid thing to have done.

58

They would never suck him in that way again.

'Come here, kid, I got something for you.' Then *wham* and he lit on his hands and knees beside the track.

Nick rubbed his eye. There was a big bump coming up. He would have a black eye, all right. It ached already. That son of a crutting brakeman.

He touched the bump over his eye with his fingers. Oh, well, it was only a black eye. That was all he had gotten out of it. Cheap at the price. He wished he could see it. Could not see it looking into the water, though. It was dark and he was a long way off from anywhere. He wiped his hands on his trousers and stood up, then climbed the embankment to the rails.

He started up the track. It was well ballasted and made easy walking, sand and gravel packed between the ties, solid walking. The smooth roadbed like a causeway went on ahead through the swamp. Nick walked along. He must get to somewhere.

Nick had swung on to the freight train when it slowed down for the yards outside of Walton Junction. The train, with Nick on it, had passed through Kalkaska as it started to get dark. Now he must be nearly to Mancelona. Three or four miles of swamp. He stepped along the track, walking so he kept on the ballast between the ties, the swamp ghostly in the rising mist. His eye ached and he was hungry. He kept on hiking, putting the miles of track back of him. The swamp was all the same on both sides of the track.

Ahead there was a bridge. Nick crossed it, his boots ringing hollow on the iron. Down below the water showed black between the slits of ties. Nick kicked a loose spike and it dropped into the water. Beyond the bridge were hills. It was high and dark on both sides of the track. Up the track Nick saw a fire.

He came up the track toward the fire carefully. It was off to one side of the track, below the railway embankment. He had only seen the light from it. The track came out through a cut and where the fire was burning the country opened out and fell away into woods. Nick dropped carefully down the embankment and cut into the woods to come up to the fire through the trees. There was a man sitting by it. Nick waited behind the tree and watched. The man looked to be alone. He was sitting there with his head in his hands looking at the fire. Nick stepped out and walked into the firelight.

The man sat there looking into the fire. When Nick stepped quite close to him he did not move.

'Hello!' Nick said.

The man looked up.

'Where did you get the shiner?' he said.

'A brakeman busted me.'

'Off the through freight?'

'Yes.'

'I saw the bastard,' the man said. 'He went through here 'bout an hour and a half ago. He was walking along the tip of the cars slapping his arms and singing.'

'The bastard!'

'It must have made him feel good to bust you,' the man said seriously.

'I'll bust him.'

'Get him with a rock sometime when he's going through,' the man advised.

'I'll get him.'

'You're a tough one, aren't you?'

'No,' Nick answered.

'All you kids are tough.'

'You got to be tough,' Nick said.

'That's what I said.'

The man looked at Nick and smiled. In the firelight Nick saw that his face was misshapen. His nose was sunken, his eyes were slits, he had queer-shaped lips. Nick did not perceive all this at once, he only saw the man's face was queerly formed and mutilated. It was like putty in colour. Dead looking in the firelight.

'Don't you like my pan?' the man asked.

Nick was embarrassed.

'Sure,' he said.

'Look here!' the man took off his cap.

He had only one ear. It was thickened and tight against the side of his head. Where the other ear should have been there was a stump.

60

'Ever seen one like that?'

'No,' said Nick. It made him a little sick.

'I could take it,' the man said. 'Don't you think I could take it, kid?'

'You bet!'

'They all bust their hands on me,' the little man said. 'They couldn't hurt me.'

He looked at Nick. 'Sit down,' he said. 'Want to eat?'

'Don't bother,' Nick said. 'I'm going on to the town.'

'Listen!' the man said. 'Call me Ad.'

'Sure!'

'Listen,' the little man said. 'I'm not quite right.'

'What's the matter?'

'I'm crazy.'

He put on his cap. Nick felt like laughing.

'You're all right,' he said.

'No, I'm not. I'm crazy. Listen, you ever been crazy?'

'No,' Nick said. 'How does it get you?'

'I don't know,' Ad said. 'When you got it you don't know about it. You know me, don't you?'

'No.'

'I'm Ad Francis.'

'Honest to God?'

'Don't you believe it?'

'Yes.'

Nick knew it must be true.

'You know how I beat them?'

'No,' Nick said.

'My heart's slow. It only beats forty a minute. Feel it.'

Nick hesitated.

'Come on,' the man took hold of his hand. 'Take hold of my wrist. Put your fingers there.'

The little man's wrist was thick and the muscles bulged above the bone. Nick felt the slow pumping under his fingers.

'Got a watch?'

'No.'

'Neither have I,' Ad said. 'It ain't any good if you haven't got a watch.'

Nick dropped his wrist.

'Listen,' Ad Francis said. 'Take ahold again. You count and I'll count up to sixty.'

Feeling the slow hard throb under his fingers, Nick started to count. He heard the little man counting slowly, one, two, three, four, five, and on – aloud.

'Sixty,' Ad finished. 'That's a minute. What did you make it?'

'Forty,' Nick said.

'That's right,' Ad said happily. 'She never speeds up.'

A man dropped down the railroad embankment and came across the clearing to the fire.

'Hello, Bugs!' Ad said.

'Hello!' Bugs answered. It was a Negro's voice. Nick knew from the way he walked that he was a Negro. He stood with his back to them, bending over the fire. He straightened up.

'This is my pal Bugs,' Ad said. 'He's crazy too.'

'Glad to meet you,' Bugs said. 'Where you say you're from?'

'Chicago,' Nick said.

'That's a fine town,' the Negro said. 'I didn't catch your name.'

'Adams. Nick Adams.'

'He says he's never been crazy, Bugs,' Ad said.

'He's got a lot coming to him,' the Negro said. He was unwrapping a package by the fire.

'When are we going to eat, Bugs?' the prizefighter asked.

'Right away.'

'Are you hungry, Nick?'

'Hungry as hell.'

'Hear that, Bugs?'

'I hear most of what goes on.'

'That ain't what I asked you.'

'Yes. I hear what the gentleman said.'

Into a skillet he was laying slices of ham. As the skillet grew hot the grease sputtered and Bugs, crouching on long nigger legs over the fire, turned the ham and broke eggs into the skillet, tipping it from side to side to baste the eggs with the hot fat.

'Will you cut some bread out of that bag, Mister Adams?' Bugs turned from the fire.

'Sure.'

Nick reached in the bag and brought out a loaf of bread. He cut six slices. Ad watched him and leaned forward.

'Let me take your knife, Nick,' he said.

'No, you don't,' the Negro said. 'Hang on to your knife, Mister Adams.'

The prizefighter sat back.

'Will you bring me the bread, Mister Adams?' Bugs asked. Nick brought it over.

'Do you like to dip your bread in the ham fat?' the Negro asked.

'You bet!'

'Perhaps we'd better wait until later. It's better at the finish of the meal. Here.'

The Negro picked up a slice of ham and laid it on one of the pieces of bread, then slid an egg on top of it.

'Just close the sandwich, will you, please, and give it to Mister Francis.'

Ad took the sandwich and started eating.

'Watch out how that egg runs,' the Negro warned. 'This is for you, Mister Adams. The remainder for myself.'

Nick bit into the sandwich. The Negro was sitting opposite him beside Ad. The hot fried ham and eggs tasted wonderful.

'Mister Adams is right hungry,' the Negro said. The little man whom Nick knew by name as a former champion fighter was silent. He had said nothing since the Negro had spoken about the knife.

'May I offer you a slice of bread dipped right in the hot ham fat?' Bugs said.

'Thanks a lot.'

The little white man looked at Nick.

'Will you have some, Mister Adolph Francis?' Bugs offered from the skillet.

Ad did not answer. He was looking at Nick.

'Mister Francis,' came the nigger's soft voice.

Ad did not answer. He was looking at Nick.

'I spoke to you, Mister Francis,' the nigger said softly.

Ad kept looking at Nick. He had his cap down over his eyes. Nick felt nervous.

63

'How the hell do you get that way?' came out from under the cap sharply at Nick. 'Who the hell do you think you are? You're a snotty bastard. You come in here where nobody asks you and eat a man's food and when he asks to borrow a knife you get snotty.'

He glared at Nick, his face was white and his eyes almost out of sight under the cap.

'You're a hot sketch. Who the hell asked you to butt in here?'

'Nobody.'

'You're damn right nobody did. Nobody asked you to stay either. You come in here and act snotty about my face and smoke my cigars and drink my liquor and then talk snotty. Where the hell do you think you get off?'

Nick said nothing. Ad stood up.

'I'll tell you, you yellow-livered Chicago bastard. You're going to get your can knocked off. Do you get that?'

Nick stepped back. The little man came toward him slowly, stepping flat-footed forward, his left foot stepping forward, his right dragging up to it.

'Hit me,' he moved his head. 'Try and hit me.'

'I don't want to hit you.'

'You don't get out of it that way. You're going to take a beating, see? Come on and lead at me.'

'Cut it out,' Nick said.

'All right then, you bastard.'

The little man looked down at Nick's feet. As he looked down the Negro, who had followed behind him as he moved away from the fire, set himself and tapped him across the base of the skull. He fell forward and Bugs dropped the cloth-wrapped blackjack on the grass. The little man lay there, his face in the grass. The Negro picked him up, his head hanging, and carried him to the fire. His face looked bad, the eyes open. Bugs laid him down gently.

'Will you bring me the water in the bucket, Mister Adams?' he said. 'I'm afraid I hit him just a little hard.'

The Negro splashed water with his hand on the man's face and pulled his ear gently. The eyes closed.

Bugs stood up.

'He's all right,' he said. 'There's nothing to worry about. I'm sorry, Mister Adams.'

'It's all right.' Nick was looking down at the little man. He saw the blackjack on the grass and picked it up. It had a flexible handle and was limber in his hand. It was made of worn black leather with a handkerchief wrapped around the heavy end.

'That's a whalebone handle,' the Negro smiled. 'They don't make them any more. I didn't know how well you could take care of yourself and, anyway, I didn't want you to hurt him or mark him up no more than he is.'

The Negro smiled again.

'You hurt him yourself.'

'I know how to do it. He won't remember nothing of it. I have to do it to change him when he gets that way.'

Nick was still looking down at the little man, lying, his eyes closed in the firelight. Bugs put some wood on the fire.

'Don't you worry about him none, Mister Adams, I seen him like this plenty of times before.'

'What makes him crazy?' Nick asked.

'Oh, a lot of things,' the Negro answered from the fire. 'Would you like a cup of this coffee, Mister Adams?'

He handed Nick the cup and smoothed the coat he had placed under the unconscious man's head.

'He took too many beatings, for one thing,' the Negro sipped the coffee. 'But that just made him sort of simple. Then his sister was his manager and they was always being written up in the papers all about brothers and sisters and how she loved her brother and how he loved his sister, and then they got married in New York and that made a lot of unpleasantness.'

'I remember about it.'

'Sure. Of course they wasn't brother and sister no more than a rabbit, but there was a lot of people didn't like it either way and they commenced to have disagreements, and one day she just went off and never came back.'

He drank his coffee and wiped his lips with the pink palm of his hand.

'He just went crazy. Will you have some more coffee, Mister Adams?'

'Thanks.'

'I seen her a couple of times,' the Negro went on. 'She was an awful good-looking woman. Looked enough like him to be twins. He wouldn't be bad-looking without his face all busted.'

He stopped. The story seemed to be over.

'Where did you meet him?' asked Nick.

'I met him in jail,' the Negro said. 'He was busting people all the time after she went away and they put him in jail. I was in for cuttin' a man.'

He smiled, and went on soft-voiced:

'Right away I liked him and when I got out I looked him up. He likes to think I'm crazy and I don't mind. I like to be with him and I like seeing the country and I don't have to commit no larceny to do it. I like living like a gentleman.'

'What do you all do?' Nick asked.

'Oh, nothing. Just move around. He's got money.'

'He must have made a lot of money.'

'Sure. He spent all his money, though. Or they took it away from him. She sends him money.'

He poked the fire.

'She's a mighty fine woman,' he said. 'She looks enough like him to be his own twin.'

The Negro looked over at the little man, lying breathing heavily. His blond hair was down over his forehead. His mutilated face looked childish in repose.

'I can wake him up any time now, Mister Adams. If you don't mind I wish you'd sort of pull out. I don't like to not be hospitable, but it might disturb him back again to see you. I hate to have to thump him and it's the only thing to do when he gets started. I have to sort of keep him away from people. You don't mind, do you, Mister Adams? No, don't thank me, Mister Adams. I'd have warned you about him but he seemed to have taken such a liking to you and I thought things were going to be all right. You'll hit a town about two miles up the track. Mancelona they call it. Good-bye. I wish we could ask you to stay the night but it's just out of the question. Would you like to take some of that ham and some bread with you? No? You better take a sandwich,' all this in a low, smooth polite nigger voice.

'Good. Well, good-bye, Mister Adams. Good-bye and good luck!'

Nick walked away from the fire across the clearing to the railway tracks. Out of the range of the fire he listened. The low soft voice of the Negro was talking. Nick could not hear the words. Then he heard the little man say, 'I got an awful headache, Bugs.'

'You'll feel better, Mister Francis,' the Negro's voice soothed. 'Just drink a cup of this hot coffee.'

Nick climbed the embankment and started up the track. He found he had a ham sandwich in his hand and put it in his pocket. Looking back from the mounting grade before the track curved into the hills he could see the firelight in the clearing.

A Very Short Story

Nick sat against the wall of the church where they had dragged
him to be clear of machine-gun fire in the street. Both legs stuck
out awkwardly. He had been hit in the spine. His face was sweaty
and dirty. The sun shone on his face. The day was very hot.
Rinaldi, big backed, his equipment sprawling, lay face down-
ward against the wall. Nick looked straight ahead brilliantly.
The pink wall of the house opposite had fallen out from the roof,
and an iron bedstead hung twisted toward the street. Two
Austrian dead lay in the rubble in the shade of the house. Up the
street were other dead. Things were getting forward in the town.
It was going well. Stretcher-bearers would be along any time now.
Nick turned his head carefully and looked at Rinaldi. 'Senta
Rinaldi. Senta. You and me we've made a separate peace.'
Rinaldi lay still in the sun breathing with difficulty. 'Not
patriots.' Nick turned his head carefully away smiling sweatily.
Rinaldi was a disappointing audience.

One very hot evening in Padua they carried him up on to the
roof and he could look out over the top of the town. There
were chimney swifts in the sky. After a while it got dark and the
searchlights came out. The others went down and took the
bottles with them. He and Luz could hear them below on the
balcony. Luz sat on the bed. She was cool and fresh in the hot
night.

Luz stayed on night-duty for three months. They were glad
to let her. When they operated on him she prepared him for

the operating table; and they had a joke about friend or enema. He went under the anaesthetic holding tight on to himself so he would not blab about anything during the silly, talky time. After he got on crutches he used to take the temperatures so Luz would not have to get up from the bed. There were only a few patients, and they all knew about it. They all liked Luz. As he walked back along the halls he thought of Luz in his bed.

Before he went back to the front they went into the Duomo and prayed. It was dim and quiet, and there were other people praying. They wanted to get married, but there was not enough time for the banns, and neither of them had birth certificates. They felt as though they were married, but they wanted everyone to know about it, and to make it so they could not lose it.

Luz wrote him many letters that he never got until after the armistice. Fifteen came in a bunch to the front and he sorted them by dates and read them all straight through. They were all about the hospital, and how much she loved him and how it was impossible to get along without him and how terrible it was missing him at night.

After the armistice they agreed he should go home to get a job so they might be married. Luz would not come home until he had a good job and could come to New York to meet her. It was understood he would not drink, and he did not want to see his friends or anyone in the States. Only to get a job and be married. On the train from Padua to Milan they quarrelled about her not being willing to come home at once. When they said good-bye, in the station at Milan, they kissed good-bye, but were not finished with the quarrel. He felt sick about saying good-bye like that.

He went to America on a boat from Genoa. Luz went back to Pordonone to open a hospital. It was lonely and rainy there and there was a battalion of *arditi* quartered in the town. Living in the muddy, rainy town in the winter, the major of the battalion made love to Luz, and she had never known Italians before, and finally wrote to the States that theirs had been only a boy-and-girl affair. She was sorry, and she knew he would probably not be able to understand, but might some day forgive her, and be grateful to her, and she expected, absolutely unexpectedly, to be married in the spring. She loved him as always, but she realized now it was only a boy-and-girl love. She hoped he would have a great career, and believed in him absolutely. She knew it was for the best.

The major did not marry her in the spring, or any other time. Luz never got an answer to the letter to Chicago about it. A short time after he contracted gonorrhoea from a sales girl in a loop department store while riding in a taxicab through Lincoln Park.

Soldier's Home

While the bombardment was knocking the trench to pieces at Fossalta, he lay very flat and sweated and prayed oh jesus christ get me out of here. Dear jesus please get me out. Christ please please please christ. If you'll only keep me from getting killed I'll do anything you say. I believe in you and I'll tell everyone in the world that you are the only one that matters. Please please dear jesus. The shelling moved farther up the line. We went to work on the trench and in the morning the sun came up and the day was hot and muggy and cheerful and quiet. The next night back at Mestre he did not tell the girl he went upstairs with at the Villa Rossa about Jesus. And he never told anybody.

Krebs went to the war from a Methodist college in Kansas. There is a picture which shows him among his fraternity brothers, all of them wearing exactly the same height and style collar. He enlisted in the Marines in 1917 and did not return to the United States until the second division returned from the Rhine in the summer of 1919.

There is a picture which shows him on the Rhine with two German girls and another corporal. Krebs and the corporal look too big for their uniforms. The German girls are not beautiful. The Rhine does not show in the picture.

By the time Krebs returned to his home town in Oklahoma the greeting of heroes was over. He came back much too late. The men from the town who had been drafted had all been welcomed elaborately on their return. There had been a great

71

deal of hysteria. Now the reaction had set in. People seemed to think it was rather ridiculous for Krebs to be getting back so late, years after the war was over.

At first Krebs, who had been at Belleau Wood, Soissons, the Champaigne, St Mihiel, and in the Argonne, did not want to talk about the war at all. Later he felt the need to talk but no one wanted to hear about it. His town had heard too many atrocity stories to be thrilled by actualities. Kreb found that to be listened to at all he had to lie, and after he had done this twice, he, too, had a reaction against the war and against talking about it. A distaste for everything that had happened to him in the war set in because of the lies he had told. All of the times that had been able to make him feel cool and clear inside himself when he thought of them; the times so long back when he had done the one thing, the only thing for a man to do, easily and naturally, when he might have done something else, now lost their cool, valuable quality and then were lost themselves.

His lies were quite unimportant lies and consisted in attributing to himself things other men had seen, done, or heard of, and stating as facts certain apocryphal incidents familiar to all soldiers. Even his lies were not sensational at the pool-room. His acquaintances who had heard detailed accounts of German women found chained to machine-guns in the Argonne forest and who could not comprehend, or were barred by their patriotism from interest in, any German machine-gunners who were not chained, were not thrilled by his stories.

Krebs acquired the nausea in regard to experience that is the result of untruth or exaggeration, and when he occasionally met another man who had really been a soldier and they talked a few minutes in the dressing-room at a dance he fell into the easy pose of the old soldier among other soldiers: that he had been badly, sickeningly frightened all the time. In this way he lost everything.

During this time, it was late summer, he was sleeping late in bed, getting up to walk down town to the library to get a book, eating lunch at home, reading on the front porch until he became bored, and then walking down through the town to spend the hottest hours of the day in the cool dark of the pool-room. He loved to play pool.

In the evening he practised on his clarinet, strolled down town, read, and went to bed. He was still a hero to his two young sisters. His mother would have given him breakfast in bed if he wanted it. She often came in when he was in bed and asked him to tell her about the war, but her attention always wandered. His father was non-committal.

Before Krebs went away to the war he had never been allowed to drive the family motor-car. His father was in the real-estate business and always wanted the car to be at his command when he required it to take clients out into the country to show them a piece of farm property. The car always stood outside the First National Bank building where his father had an office on the second floor. Now, after the war, it was still the same car.

Nothing was changed in the town except that the young girls had grown up. But they lived in such a complicated world of already defined alliances and shifting feuds that Krebs did not feel the energy or the courage to break into it. He liked to look at them, though. There were so many good-looking young girls. Most of them had their hair cut short. When he went away only little girls wore their hair like that or girls that were fast. They all wore sweaters and shirt waists with round Dutch collars. It was a pattern. He liked to look at them from the front porch as they walked on the other side of the street. He liked to watch them walking under the shade of the trees. He liked the round Dutch collars above their sweaters. He liked their stockings and flat shoes. He liked their bobbed hair and the way they walked.

When he was in town their appeal to him was not very strong. He did not like them when he saw them in the Greek's ice-cream parlour. He did not want them themselves really. They were too complicated. There was something else. Vaguely he wanted a girl but he did not want to have to work to get her. He would have liked to have a girl but he did not want to have to spend a long time getting her. He did not want to get into the intrigue and the politics. He did not want to have to do any courting. He did not want to tell any more lies. It wasn't worth it.

He did not want any consequences. He did not want any consequences ever again. He wanted to live along without consequences. Besides he did not really need a girl. The army had taught him that. It was all right to pose as though you had to have a girl. Nearly everybody did that. But it wasn't true. You did not need a girl. That was the funny thing. First a fellow boasted how girls meant nothing to him, then a fellow boasted that he could not get along without girls, that he had to have them all the time, that he could not go to sleep without them.

That was all a lie. It was all a lie both ways. You did not need a girl unless you thought about them. He learned that in the army. Then sooner or later you always got one. When you were really ripe for a girl you always got one. You did not have to think about it. Sooner or later it would come. He had learned that in the army.

Now he would have liked a girl if she had come to him and not wanted to talk. But here at home it was all too complicated. He knew he could never get through it all again. It was not worth the trouble. That was the thing about French girls and German girls. There was not all this talking. You couldn't talk much and you did not need to talk. It was simple and you were friends. He thought about France and then he began to think about Germany. On the whole he had liked Germany better. He did not want to leave Germany. He did not want to come home. Still, he had come home. He sat on the front porch.

He liked the girls that were walking along the other side of the street. He liked the look of them much better than the French girls or the German girls. But the world they were in was not the world he was in. He would like to have one of them. But it was not worth it. They were such a nice pattern. He liked the pattern. It was exciting. But he would not go through all the talking. He did not want one badly enough. He liked to look at them all, though. It was not worth it. Not now when things were getting good again.

He sat there on the porch reading a book on the war. It was a history and he was reading about all the engagements he had been in. It was the most interesting reading he had ever done. He wished there were more maps. He looked forward with a good feeling to reading all the really good histories when they would come out with good detail maps. Now he was really learning about the war. He had been a good soldier. That made a difference.

One morning after he had been home about a month his mother came into his bedroom and sat on the bed. She smoothed his apron.

'I had a talk with your father last night, Harold,' she said, 'and he is willing for you to take the car out in the evenings.'

'Yeah?' said Krebs, who was not fully awake. 'Take the car out? Yeah?'

'Yes. Your father has felt for some time that you should be able to take the car out in the evenings whenever you wished, but we only talked it over last night.'

'I'll bet you made him,' Krebs said.

'No. It was your father's suggestion that we talk the matter over.'

'Yeah. I'll bet you made him,' Krebs sat up in bed.

'Will you come down to breakfast, Harold?' his mother said.

'As soon as I get my clothes on,' Krebs said.

His mother went out of the room and he could hear her frying something downstairs while he washed, shaved, and dressed to go down into the dining-room for breakfast. While he was eating breakfast his sister brought in the mail.

'Well, Hare,' she said. 'You old sleepy-head. What do you ever get up for?'

Krebs looked at her. He liked her. She was his best sister.

'Have you got the paper?' he asked.

She handed him the *Kansas City Star* and he shucked off its brown wrapper and opened it to the sporting page. He folded the *Star* open and propped it against the water pitcher with his cereal dish to steady it, so he could read while he ate.

'Harold,' his mother stood in the kitchen doorway, 'Harold, please don't muss up the paper. Your father can't read his *Star* if it's been mussed.'

'I won't muss it,' Krebs said.

His sister sat down at the table and watched him while he read.

'We're playing indoor over at school this afternoon,' she said. 'I'm going to pitch.'

'Good,' said Krebs. 'How's the old wing?'

'I can pitch better than lots of the boys. I tell them all you taught me. The other girls aren't much good.'

'Yeah?' said Krebs.

'I tell them all you're my beau. Aren't you my beau, Hare?'

'You bet.'

'Couldn't your brother really be your beau just because he's your brother?'

'I don't know.'

'Sure you know. Couldn't you be my beau, Hare, if I was old enough and if you wanted to?'

'Sure. You're my girl now.'

'Am I really your girl?'

'Sure.'

'So you love me?'

'Uh, huh.'

'Will you always love me?'

'Sure.'

'Will you come and watch me play indoor?'

'Maybe.'

'Aw, Hare, you don't love me. If you loved me, you'd want to come over and watch me play indoor.'

Kreb's mother came into the dining-room from the kitchen. She carried a plate of two fried eggs and some crisp bacon on it and a plate of buckwheat cakes.

'You run along, Helen,' she said. 'I want to talk to Harold.'

She put the eggs and bacon down in front of him and brought in a jug of maple syrup for the buckwheat cakes. Then she sat down across the table from Krebs.

'I wish you'd put down the paper in a minute, Harold,' she said.

Krebs took down the paper and folded it.

'Have you decided what you are going to do yet, Harold?' his mother said, taking off her glasses.

'No,' said Krebs.

'Don't you think it's about time?' his mother did not say this in a mean way. She seemed worried.

'I hadn't thought about it,' Krebs said.

'God has some work for everyone to do,' his mother said.

'There can be no idle hands in His Kingdom.'

'I'm not in His Kingdom,' Krebs said.

'We are all of us in His Kingdom.'

Krebs felt embarrassed and resentful as always.

'I've worried about you so much, Harold,' his mother went on. 'I know the temptations you must have been exposed to. I know how weak men are. I know what your own dear grandfather, my own father, told us about the Civil War and I have prayed for you. I pray for you all day long, Harold.'

Krebs looked at the bacon fat hardening on his plate.

'Your father is worried, too,' his mother went on. 'He thinks you have lost your ambition, that you haven't got a definite aim in life. Charley Simmons, who is just your age, has a good job and is going to be married. The boys are all settling down; they're all determined to get somewhere; you can see that boys like Charley Simmons are on their way to being really a credit to the community.'

Krebs said nothing.

'Don't look that way, Harold,' his mother said. 'You know we love you and I want to tell you for your own good how matters stand. Your father does not want to hamper your freedom. He thinks you should be allowed to drive the car. If you want to take some of the nice girls out riding with you, we are only too pleased. We want you to enjoy yourself. But you are going to have to settle down to work, Harold. Your father doesn't care what you start in at. All work is honourable as he says. But you've got to make a start at something. He asked me to speak to you this morning and then you can stop in and see him at his office.'

'Is that all?' Krebs said.

'Yes. Don't you love your mother, dear boy?' 'No,' Krebs said.

His mother looked at him across the table. Her eyes were shiny. She started crying.

'I don't love anybody,' Kreb said.

It wasn't any good. He couldn't tell her, he couldn't make her see it. It was silly to have said it. He had only hurt her. He went over and took hold of her arm. She was crying with her head in her hands.

'I didn't mean it,' he said. 'I was just angry at something. I didn't mean I didn't love you.'

His mother went on crying. Krebs put his arm on her shoulder.

'Can't you believe me, mother?'

His mother shook her head.

'Please, please, mother. Please believe me.'

'All right,' his mother said chokily. She looked up at him. 'I believe you, Harold.'

Krebs kissed her hair. She put her face up to him.

'I'm your mother,' she said. 'I held you next to my heart when you were a tiny baby.'

Krebs felt sick and vaguely nauseated.

'I know, Mummy,' he said. 'I'll try to be a good boy for you.'

'Would you kneel and pray with me, Harold?' his mother asked.

They knelt down beside the dining-room table and Krebs's mother prayed.

'Now, you pray, Harold,' she said.

'I can't,' Krebs said.

'Try, Harold.'

'I can't.'

'Do you want me to pray for you?'

'Yes.'

So his mother prayed for him and then they stood up and Krebs kissed his mother and went out of the house. He had tried so to keep his life from being complicated. Still, none of it had touched him. He had felt sorry for his mother and she had made him lie. He would go to Kansas City and get a job and she would feel all right about it. There would be one more scene maybe before he went away. He would not go down to his father's office. He would miss that one. He wanted his life to go smoothly. It had just gotten going that way. Well, that was all over now, anyway. He would go over to the schoolyard and watch Helen play indoor baseball.

The Revolutionist

At two o'clock in the morning two Hungarians got into a cigar store at Fifteenth and Grand Avenue. Drevitts and Boyle drove up from the Fifteenth Street police station in a Ford. The Hungarians were backing their wagon out of an alley. Boyle shot one off the seat of the wagon and one out of the wagon box. Drevitts got frightened when he found they were both dead. 'Hell, Jimmy,' he said, 'you oughtn't to have done it. There's liable to be a hell of a lot of trouble.'

'They're crooks, ain't they?' said Boyle. 'They're wops, ain't they? Who the hell is going to make any trouble?'

'That's all right maybe this time,' said Drevitts, 'but how did you know they were wops when you dumped them?'

'Wops,' said Boyle, 'I can tell wops a mile off.'

In 1919 he was travelling on the railroads in Italy, carrying a square of oilcloth from the headquarters of the party written in indelible pencil and saying here was a comrade who had suffered very much under the Whites in Budapest and requesting comrades to aid him in any way. He used this instead of a ticket. He was very shy and quite young and the train men passed him on from one crew to another. He had no money, and they fed him behind the counter in railway eating-houses.

He was delighted with Italy. It was a beautiful country, he said. The people were all kind. He had been in many towns, walked much, and seen many pictures. Giotto, Masaccio, and Piero della Fancesca he bought reproductions of and carried

79

them wrapped in a copy of *Avanti*. Mantegna he did not like.

He reported at Bologna, and I took him with me up into the Romagna where it was necessary I go to see a man. We had a good trip together. It was early September and the country was pleasant. He was a Magyar, a very nice boy and very shy. Horthy's men had done some bad things to him. He talked about it a little. In spite of Hungary, he believed altogether in the world revolution.

'But how is the movement going in Italy?' he asked.

'Very badly,' I said.

'But it will go better,' he said. 'You have everything here. It is the one country that everyone is sure of. It will be the starting-point of everything.'

I did not say anything.

At Bologna he said good-bye to us to go on the train to Milano and then to Aosta to walk over the pass into Switzerland. I spoke to him about the Mantegnas in Milano. 'No,' he said, very shyly, he did not like Mantegna. I wrote out for him where to eat in Milano and the addresses of comrades. He thanked me very much, but his mind was already looking forward to walking over the pass. He was very eager to walk over the pass while the weather held good. He loved the mountains in the autumn. The last I heard of him the Swiss had him in jail near Sion.

Mr and Mrs Elliot

The first matador got the horn through his sword hand and the crowd hooted him. The second matador slipped and the bull caught him through the belly and he hung on to the horn with one hand and held the other tight against the place, and the bull rammed him wham against the wall and the horn came out, and he lay in the sand, and then got up like crazy drunk and tried to slug the men carrying him away and yelled for his sword but he fainted. The kid came out and had to kill five bulls because you can't have more than three matadors, and the last bull he was so tired he couldn't get the sword in. He couldn't hardly lift his arm. He tried five times and the crowd was quiet because it was a good bull and it looked like him or the bull and then he finally made it. He sat down in the sand and puked and they held a cape over him while the crowd hollered and threw things down into the bullring.

Mr and Mrs Elliot tried very hard to have a baby. They tried as often as Mrs Elliot could stand it. They tried in Boston after they were married and they tried coming over on the boat. They did not try very often on the boat because Mrs Elliot was quite sick. She was sick and when she was sick she was sick as Southern women are sick. That is women from the southern part of the United States. Like all Southern women Mrs Elliot disintegrated very quickly under sea sickness, travelling at night, and getting up too early in the morning. Many of the people on the boat took her for Elliot's mother. Other people who knew they were married believed she was going to have a baby. In reality she was forty years old. Her years had been precipitated suddenly when she started travelling.

She had seemed younger, in fact she had seemed not to have any age at all, when Elliot married her after several weeks of making love to her after knowing her for a long time in her tea shop before he had kissed her one evening.

Hubert Elliot was taking postgraduate work in law at Harvard when he married. He was a poet with an income of nearly ten thousand dollars a year. He wrote very long poems rapidly. He was twenty-five years old and had never gone to bed with a woman until he married Mrs Elliot. He wanted to keep himself pure so that he could bring to his wife the same purity of mind and body that he expected of her. He called it to himself living straight. He had been in love with various girls before he kissed Mrs Elliot and always told them sooner or later that he had led a clean life. Nearly all the girls lost interest in him. He was shocked and really horrified at the way girls would become engaged to and marry men whom they must know had dragged themselves through the gutter. He once tried to warn a girl he knew against a man of whom he had almost proof that he had been a rotter at college and a very unpleasant incident had resulted.

Mrs Elliot's name was Cornelia. She had taught him to call her Calutina, which was her family nickname in the South. His mother cried when he brought Cornelia home after their marriage but brightened very much when she learned they were going to live abroad.

Cornelia had said, 'You dear sweet boy,' and held him closer than ever when he had told her how he had kept himself clean for her. Cornelia was pure too. 'Kiss me again like that,' she said.

Hubert explained to her that he had learned that way of kissing from hearing a fellow tell a story once. He was delighted with his experiment and they developed it as far as possible. Sometimes when they had been kissing together a long time, Cornelia would ask him to tell her again that he had kept himself really straight for her. The declaration always set her off again.

At first Hubert had no idea of marrying Cornelia. He had

82

never thought of her that way. She had been such a good friend of his, and then one day in the little back room of the shop they had been dancing to the gramophone while her girl friend was in the front of the shop and she looked up into his eyes and he had kissed her. He could never remember just when it was decided that they were to be married. But they were married.

They spent the night of the day they were married in a Boston hotel. They were both disappointed but finally Cornelia went to sleep. Hubert could not sleep and several times went out and walked up and down the corridor of the hotel in his new Jaeger bathrobe that he had bought for his wedding trip. As he walked he saw all the pairs of shoes, small shoes and big shoes, outside the doors of the hotel rooms. This set his heart to pounding and he hurried back to his own room but Cornelia was asleep. He did not like to waken her and soon everything was quite all right and he slept peacefully.

The next day they called on his mother and the next day they sailed for Europe. It was possible to try to have a baby but Cornelia could not attempt it very often although they wanted a baby more than anything else in the world. They landed at Cherbourg and came to Paris. They tried to have a baby in Paris. Then they decided to go to Dijon where there was summer school and where a number of people who crossed the boat with them had gone. They found there was nothing to do in Dijon. Hubert, however, was writing a great number of poems and Cornelia typed them for him. They were all very long poems. He was very severe about mistakes and would make her re-do an entire page if there was one mistake. She cried a good deal and they tried several times to have a baby before they left Dijon.

They came to Paris and most of their friends from the boat came back too. They were tired of Dijon and anyway would now be able to say that after leaving Harvard or Columbia or Wabash they had studied at the University of Dijon down in the Côte d'Or. Many of them would have preferred to go to Languedoc, Montpellier, or Perpignan if there are universities there. But all those places are too far away. Dijon is only four and a half hours from Paris and there is a diner on the train.

So they all sat around the Café du Dome, avoiding the Rotonde across the street because it is always so full of foreigners for a few days and then the Elliots rented a château in Touraine through an advertisement in the New York *Herald*. Elliot had a number of friends by now all of whom admired his poetry and Mrs Elliot had prevailed upon him to send over to Boston for her girl friend who had been in the tea shop. Mrs Elliot had became much brighter after her girl friend came and they had many good cries together. The girl friend was several years older than Cornelia and called her Honey. She too came from a very old Southern family.

The three of them, with several of Elliot's friends who called him Hubie, went down to the château in Touraine. They found Touraine to be a very flat hot country very much like Kansas. Elliot had nearly enough poems for a book now. He was going to bring it out in Boston and had already sent his cheque to, and made a contract with, a publisher.

In a short time the friends began to drift back to Paris. Touraine had not turned out the way it looked when it was started. Soon all the friends had gone off with a rich young and unmarried poet to a seaside resort near Trouville. There they were all very happy.

Elliot kept on at the château in Touraine because he had taken it for all summer. He and Mrs Elliot tried very hard to have a baby in the big bedroom on the big, hard bed. Mrs Elliot was learning the touch system on the typewriter, but she found that while it increased the speed it made more mistakes. The girl friend was now typing practically all of the manuscripts. She was very neat and efficient and seemed to enjoy it.

Elliot had taken to drinking white wine and lived apart in his own room. He wrote a great deal of poetry during the night and in the morning looked very exhausted. Mrs Elliot and the girl friend now slept together in the big medieval bed. They had many a good cry together. In the evening they all sat at dinner together in the garden under a plane tree and the evening wind blew and Elliot drank white wine and Mrs Elliot and the girl friend made conversation and they were all quite happy

Cat in the Rain

*They whack-whacked the white horse on the legs and he kneed
himself up. The picador twisted the stirrups straight and pulled
and hauled up into the saddle. The horse's entrails hung down in
a blue bunch and swung backward and forward as he began to
canter, the* monos *whacking him on the back of his legs with the
rods. He cantered jerkily along the* barrera. *He stopped stiff and
one of the* monos *held his bridle and walked him forward. The
picador kicked in his spurs, leaned forward, and shook his lance
at the bull. Blood pumped regularly from between the horse's
front legs. He was nervously wobbly. The bull could not make up
his mind to charge.*

There were only two Americans stopping at the hotel. They
did not know any of the people they passed on the stairs on
their way to and from their room. Their room was on the
second floor facing the sea. It also faced the public garden and
the war monument. There were big palms and green benches
in the public garden. In the good weather there was always an
artist with his easel. Artists liked the way the palms grew and
the bright colours of the hotels facing the gardens and the sea.
Italians came from a long way off to look up at the war monument. It was made of bronze and glistened in the rain. It was
raining. The rain dripped from the palm trees. Water stood in
pools on the gravel paths. The sea broke in a long line in the
rain and slipped back down the beach to come up and break
again in a long line in the rain. The motor-cars were gone from

the square by the war monument. Across the square in the doorway of the café a waiter stood looking out at the empty square.

The American wife stood at the window looking out. Outside right under their window a cat was crouched under one of the dripping green tables. The cat was trying to make herself so compact that she would not be dripped on.

'I'm going down and get that kitty,' the American wife said.

'I'll do it,' her husband offered from the bed.

'No, I'll get it. The poor kitty out trying to keep dry under a table.'

The husband went on reading, lying propped up with the two pillows at the foot of the bed.

'Don't get wet,' he said.

The wife went downstairs and the hotel owner stood up and bowed to her as she passed the office. His desk was at the far end of the office. He was an old man and very tall.

'*Il piove*,' the wife said. She liked the hotel-keeper.

'*Si, si, Signora, brutto tempo*. It's very bad weather.'

He stood behind his desk in the far end of the dim room. The wife liked him. She liked the deadly serious way he received any complaints. She liked his dignity. She liked the way he wanted to serve her. She liked the way he felt about being a hotel-keeper. She liked his old, heavy face and big hands.

Liking him she opened the door and looked out. It was raining harder. A man in a rubber cape was crossing the empty square to the café. The cat would be around to the right. Perhaps she could go along under the eaves. As she stood in the doorway an umbrella opened behind her. It was the maid who looked after their room.

'You must not get wet,' she smiled, speaking Italian. Of course, the hotel-keeper had sent her.

With the maid holding the umbrella over her, she walked along the gravel path until she was under their window. The table was there, washed bright green in the rain, but the cat was gone. She was suddenly disappointed. The maid looked up at her.

'*Ha perduto qualchecosa, Signora?*'

'There was a cat?' said the American girl.

'A cat?'

'*Si, il gatto.*'

'A cat?' the maid laughed. 'A cat in the rain?'

'Yes,' she said, 'under the table.' Then, 'Oh, I wanted it so much. I wanted a kitty.'

When she talked English the maid's face tightened.

'Come, *Signora*,' she said. 'We must get back inside. You will be wet.'

'I suppose so,' said the American girl.

They went back along the gravel path and passed in the door. The maid stayed outside to close the umbrella. As the American girl passed the office, the *padrone* bowed from his desk. Something felt very small and tight inside the girl. The *padrone* made her feel small and at the same time really important. She had a momentary feeling of being of supreme importance. She went on up the stairs. She opened the door of the room. George was on the bed, reading.

'Did you get the cat?' he asked, putting the book down.

'It was gone.'

'Wonder where it went to?' he said, resting his eyes from reading.

She sat down on the bed.

'I wanted it so much,' she said. 'I don't know why I wanted it so much. I wanted that poor kitty. It isn't any fun to be a poor kitty out in the rain.'

George was reading again.

She went over and sat in front of the mirror of the dressing-table looking at herself with the hand glass. She studied her profile, first one side and then the other. Then she studied the back of her head and her neck.

'Don't you think it would be a good idea if I let my hair grow out?' she asked, looking at her profile again.

George looked up and saw the back of her neck, clipped close like a boy's.

'I like it the way it is.'

'I get so tired of it,' she said. 'I get so tired of looking like a boy.'

George shifted his position in the bed. He hadn't looked away from her since she started to speak.

'You look pretty darn nice,' he said.

She laid the mirror down on the dresser and went over to the window and looked out. It was getting dark.

'I want to pull my hair back tight and smooth and make a big knot at the back that I can feel,' she said. 'I want to have a kitty to sit on my lap and purr when I stroke her.'

'Yeah?' George said from the table.

'And I want to eat at a table with my own silver and I want candles. And I want it to be spring and I want to brush my hair out in front of a mirror and I want a kitty and I want some new clothes.'

'Oh, shut up and get something to read,' George said. He was reading again.

His wife was looking out of the window. It was quite dark now and still raining in the palm trees.

'Anyway, I want a cat,' she said. 'I want a cat. I want a cat now. If I can't have long hair or any fun, I want a cat.'

George was not listening. He was reading his book. His wife looked out of the window where the light had come on in the square.

Someone knocked at the door.

'*Avanti*,' George said. He looked up from his book.

In the doorway stood the maid. She held a big tortoiseshell cat pressed tight against her and swung down against her body.

'Excuse me,' she said, 'the *padrone* asked me to bring this for the *Signora*.'

Out of Season

The crowd shouted all the time and threw pieces of bread down into the ring, then cushions and leather wine bottles, keeping up whistling and yelling. Finally the bull was too tired from so much bad sticking and folded his knees and lay down and one of the cuadrilla *leaned out over his neck and killed him with the* puntilla. *The crowd came over the barrera and around the torero and two men grabbed him and held him and someone cut off his pigtail and was waving it and a kid grabbed it and ran away with it. Afterwards I saw him at the café. He was very short with a brown face and quite drunk and he said after all it has happened before like that. I am not really a good bull-fighter.*

On the four lire Peduzzi had earned by spading the hotel garden he got quite drunk. He saw the young gentleman coming down the path and spoke to him mysteriously. The young gentleman said he had not eaten but would be ready to go as soon as lunch had finished. Forty minutes or an hour.

At the *cantina* near the bridge they trusted him for three more grappas because he was so confident and mysterious about his job for the afternoon. It was a windy day with the sun coming out from behind the clouds and then going under in sprinkles of rain. A wonderful day for trout fishing.

The young gentleman came out of the hotel and asked him about the rods. Should his wife come behind with the rods? 'Yes,' said Peduzzi, 'let her follow us.' The young gentleman went back into the hotel and spoke to his wife. He and Peduzzi started down the road. The young gentleman had a musette over his shoulder. Peduzzi saw the wife, who looked as young as the young gentleman, and was wearing mountain boots and a blue beret, start out to follow them down the road, carrying the fishing rods, unjointed, one in each hand. Peduzzi didn't like her to be way back there. '*Signorina*,' he called, winking at the young gentleman, 'come up here and walk with us. *Signora*, come up here. Let us all walk together.' Peduzzi wanted them all three to walk down the street of Cortina together.

The wife stayed behind, following rather sullenly. '*Signora*,' Peduzzi called tenderly, 'come up here with us.' The young gentleman looked back and shouted something. The wife stopped lagging behind and walked up.

Everyone they met walking through the main street of the town Peduzzi greeted elaborately. *Buon' di, Arturo!* Tipping his hat. The bank clerk stared at him from the door of the Fascist café. Groups of three and four people standing in front of the shops stared at the three. The workmen in their stone-powdered jackets working on the foundations of the new hotel looked up as they passed. Nobody spoke or gave any sign to them except the town beggar, lean and old, with a spittle-thickened beard, who lifted his hat as they passed.

Peduzzi stopped in front of a store with the window full of bottles and brought his empty grappa bottle from an inside pocket of his old military coat. 'A little to drink, some marsala for the *Signora*, something, something to drink.' He gestured with the bottle. It was a wonderful day. 'Marsala, you like marsala, *Signora*? A little marsala?'

The wife stood sullenly. 'You'll have to play up to this,' she said. 'I can't understand a word he says. He's drunk, isn't he?'

The young gentleman appeared not to hear Peduzzi. He was thinking, what in the hell makes him say marsala? That's what Max Beerbohm drinks.

'Geld,' Peduzzi said finally, taking hold of the young gentleman's sleeve. 'Lire.' He smiled, reluctant to press the subject but needing to bring the young gentleman into action.

The young gentleman took out his pocketbook and gave him a ten-lire note. Peduzzi went up the steps to the door of

90

the Specialty of Domestic and Foreign Wines shop. It was locked.

'It is closed until two,' someone passing in the street said scornfully. Peduzzi came down the steps. He felt hurt. 'Never mind,' he said, 'we can get it at the Concordia.'

They walked down the road to the Concordia three abreast. On the porch of the Concordia, where the rusty bobsleds were stacked, the young gentleman said, '*Was wollen Sie?*' Peduzzi handed him the ten-lire note folded over and over. 'Nothing,' he said, 'anything.' He was embarrassed. 'Marsala, maybe. I don't know. Marsala?'

The door of the Concordia shut on the young gentleman and the wife. 'Three marsalas,' said the young gentleman to the girl behind the pastry counter. 'Two, you mean?' she asked. 'No,' he said, 'One for a *vecchio*.' 'Oh,' she said, 'a *vecchio*,' and laughed, getting down the bottle. She poured out three muddy-looking drinks into three glasses. The wife was sitting at a table under the line of newspapers on sticks. 'You might as well drink it,' he said, 'maybe it'll make you feel better.' She sat and looked at the glass. The young gentleman went outside the door with a glass for Peduzzi but could not see him.

'I don't know where he is,' he said, coming back into the pastry room carrying the glass.

'He wanted a quart of it,' said the wife.

'How much is a quarter litre?' the young gentleman asked the girl.

'Of the bianco? One lira.'

'No, of the marsala. Put these two in, too,' he said, giving her his own glass and the one poured for Peduzzi. She filled the quarter-litre wine measure with a funnel. 'A bottle to carry it,' said the young gentleman.

She went to hunt for a bottle. It all amused her.

'I'm sorry you feel so rotten, Tiny,' he said. 'I'm sorry I talked the way I did at lunch. We were both getting at the same thing from different angles.'

'It doesn't make any difference,' she said. 'None of it makes any difference.'

'Are you too cold?' he asked. 'I wish you'd worn another sweater.'

'I've got on three sweaters.'

The girl came in with a very slim brown bottle and poured the marsala into it. The young gentleman paid five lire more. They went out the door. The girl was amused. Peduzzi was walking up and down at the other end out of the wind and holding rods.

'Come on,' he said. 'I will carry the rods. What difference does it make if anybody sees them? No one will trouble us. No one will make any trouble for me in Cortina. I know them at the *municipio*. I have been a soldier. Everybody in this town likes me. I sell frogs. What if it is forbidden to fish? Not a thing. Nothing. No trouble. Big trout, I tell you. Lots of them.'

They were walking down the hill toward the river. The town was in back of them. The sun had gone under and it was sprinkling rain. 'There,' said Peduzzi, pointing to a girl in the doorway of a house they passed. 'My daughter.'

'His doctor,' the wife said, 'has he got to show us his doctor?'

'He said his daughter,' said the young gentleman.

The girl went into the house as Peduzzi pointed.

They walked down the hill across the fields and then turned to follow the river bank. Peduzzi talked rapidly with much winking and knowingness. As they walked three abreast the wife caught his breath across the wind. Once he nudged her in the ribs. Part of the time he talked in d'Ampezzo dialect and sometimes in Tyroler German dialect. He could not make out which the young gentleman and his wife understood the best so he was being bilingual. But as the young gentleman said, *Ja, Ja*, Peduzzi decided to talk altogether in Tyroler. The young gentleman and the wife understood nothing.

'Everybody in the town saw us going through with these rods. We're probably being followed by the game police now. I wish we weren't in on this damn thing. This damned old fool is so drunk, too.'

'Of course you haven't got the guts to just go back,' said the wife. 'Of course you have to go on.'

'Why don't you go back? Go on back, Tiny.'

'I'm going to stay with you. If you go to jail we might as well both go.'

They turned sharp down the bank and Peduzzi stood, his coat blowing in the wind, gesturing at the river. It was brown and muddy. Off on the right there was a dump heap.

'Say it to me in Italian,' said the young gentleman.

'*Un' mezz'ora. Più d'un' mezz'ora.*'

'He says it's at least a half-hour more. Go on back, Tiny. You're cold in this wind anyway. It's a rotten day and we aren't going to have any fun, anyway.'

'All right,' she said, and climbed up the grassy bank.

Peduzzi was down at the river and did not notice her till she was almost out of sight over the crest. '*Frau!*' he shouted. '*Frau! Fraülein!* You're not going.'

She went on over the crest of the hill.

'She's gone!' said Peduzzi. It shocked him.

He took off the rubber bands that held the rod segments together and commenced to joint up one of the rods.

'But you said it was half an hour farther.'

'Oh, yes. It is good half an hour down. It is good here, too.'

'Really?'

'Of course. It is good here and good there, too.'

The young gentleman sat down on the bank and jointed up a rod, put on the reel, and threaded the line through the guides. He felt uncomfortable and afraid that any minute a gamekeeper or a posse of citizens would come over the bank from the town. He could see the houses of the town and the campanile over the edge of the hill. He opened his leather box. Peduzzi leaned over and dug his flat, hard thumb and forefinger in and tangled the moistened leaders.

'Have you some lead?'

'No.'

'You must have some lead.' Peduzzi was excited. 'You must have *piombo. Piombo.* A little *piombo.* Just here. Just above the hook or your bait will float on the water. You must have it. Just a little *piombo.*'

'Have you got some?'

'No.' He looked through his pockets desperately, sifting through the cloth dirt in the lining of his inside military pockets. 'I haven't any. We must have *piombo.*'

'We can't fish then,' said the young gentleman, and unjointed

93

the rod, reeling the line through the guides. 'We'll get some *piombo* and fish tomorrow.'

'But listen, *caro*, you must have *piombo*. The line will lie flat on the water.' Peduzzi's day was going to pieces before his eyes. 'You must have *piombo*. A little is enough. Your stuff is all clean and new but you have no lead. I would have brought some. You said you had everything.'

The young gentleman looked at the stream discoloured by the melting snow. 'I know,' he said, 'we'll get some *piombo* and fish tomorrow.'

'At what hour in the morning? Tell me that?'

'At seven.'

The sun came out. It was warm and pleasant. The young gentleman felt relieved. He was no longer breaking the law. Sitting on the bank he took the bottle of marsala out of his pocket and passed it to Peduzzi. Peduzzi passed it back. The young gentleman took a drink of it and passed it to Peduzzi again. Peduzzi passed it back again. 'Drink,' he said, "drink. It's your marsala.' After another short drink the young gentleman handed the bottle over. Peduzzi had been watching it closely. He took the bottle very hurriedly and tipped it up. The grey hairs in the folds of his neck oscillated as he drank, his eyes fixed on the end of the narrow brown bottle. He drank it all. The sun shone while he drank. It was wonderful. This was a great day, after all. A wonderful day.

'*Senta, caro!* In the morning at seven.' He had called the young gentleman *caro* several times and nothing had happened. It was good marsala. His eyes glistened. Days like this stretched out ahead. It would begin at seven in the morning.

They started to walk up the hill toward the town. The young gentleman went on ahead. He was quite a way up the hill. Peduzzi called to him.

'Listen, *caro*, can you let me take five lire for a favour?'

'For today?' asked the young gentleman frowning.

'No, not today. Give it to me today for tomorrow. I will provide everything for tomorrow. Pane, salami, formaggio, good stuff for all of us. You and I and the *Signora*. Bait for fishing, minnows, not worms only. Perhaps I can get some marsala. All for five lire. Five lire for a favour.'

The young gentleman looked through his pocketbook and took out a two-lire note and two ones.

'Thank you, *caro*. Thank you,' said Peduzzi, in the tone of one member of the Carlton Club accepting the *Morning Post* from another. This was living. He was through with the hotel garden, breaking up frozen manure with a dung fork. Life was opening out.

'Until seven o'clock then, *caro*,' he said, slapping the young gentleman on the back. 'Promptly at seven.'

'I may not be going,' said the young gentleman putting his purse back in his pocket.

'What,' said Peduzzi, 'I will have minnows, *Signor*. Salami, everything. You and I and the *Signora*. The three of us.'

'I may not be going,' said the young gentleman, 'very probably not. I will leave word with the *padrone* at the hotel office.'

Cross-Country Snow

If it happened right down close in front of you, you could see Villalta snarl at the bull and curse him, and when the bull charged he swung back firmly like an oak when the wind hits it, his legs tight together, the muleta trailing and the sword following the curve behind. Then he cursed the bull, flopped the muleta at him, and swung back from the charge, his feet firm, the muleta curving, and at each swing the crowd rearing.

When he started to kill it was all in the same rush. The bull looking at him straight in front, hating. He drew out the sword from the folds of the muleta and sighted with the same movement and called to the bull, 'Toro! Toro!' and the bull charged and Villalta charged and just for a moment they became one. Villalta became one with the bull and then it was over. Villalta standing straight and the red hilt of the sword sticking out dully between the bull's shoulders. Villalta, his hand up at the crowd and the bull roaring blood, looking straight at Villalta and his legs caving.

The funicular car bucked once more and then stopped. It could not go farther, the snow drifted solidly across the track. The gale scouring the exposed surface of the mountain had swept the snow surface into a wind-board crust. Nick, waxing his skis in the baggage car, pushed his boots into the toe irons and shut the clamp tight. He jumped from the car sideways on to the hard wind-board, made a jump turn, and crouching and trailing his sticks slipped in a rush down the slope.

On the white below George dipped and rose and dipped out of sight. The rush and the sudden swoop as he dropped down a steep undulation in the mountainside plucked Nick's mind out and left him only the wonderful flying, dropping sensation in his body. He rose to a slight up-run and then the snow seemed to drop out from under him as he went down, down, faster and faster in a rush down the last, long steep slope. Crouching so he was almost sitting back on his skis, trying to keep the centre of gravity low, the snow driving like a sandstorm, he knew the pace was too much. But he held it. He would not let go and spill. Then a patch of soft snow, left in a hollow by the wind, spilled him and he went over and over in a clashing of skis, feeling like a shot rabbit, then stuck, his legs crossed, his skis sticking straight up and his nose and ears jammed full of snow.

George stood a little farther down the slope, knocking the snow from his wind jacket with big slaps.

'You took a beauty, Mike,' he called to Nick. 'That's lousy soft snow. It bagged me the same way.'

'What's it like over the khud?' Nick kicked his skis around as he lay on his back and stood up.

'You've got to keep to your left. It's a good fast drop with a Christy at the bottom on account of a fence.'

'Wait a sec and we'll take it together.'

'No, you come on and go first. I like to see you take the khuds.'

Nick Adams came up past George, big back and blond head still faintly snowy, then his skis started slipping at the edge and he swooped down, hissing in the crystalline powder snow and seeming to float up and down as he went up and down the billowing khuds. He held to his left at the end, as he rushed toward the fence, keeping his knees locked tight together and turning his body like tightening a screw brought his skis sharply around to the right in a smother of snow and slowed into a loss of speed parallel to the hillside and the wire fence.

He looked up the hill. George was coming down in telemark position, kneeling; one leg forward and bent, the other trailing; his sticks hanging like some insect's thin legs, kicking up puffs of snow as they touched the surface and finally the whole kneeling, trailing figure coming around in a beautiful right curve, crouching, the legs shot forward and back, the body leaning out against the swing, the sticks accenting the curve like points of light, all in a wild cloud of snow.

'I was afraid to Christy,' George said, 'the snow was too deep. You made a beauty.'

'I can't telemark with my leg,' Nick said.

Nick held down the top strand of the wire fence with his ski and George slid over. Nick followed him down the road. They thrust bent-kneed along the road into a pine forest. The road became polished ice, stained orange and a tobacco yellow from the teams hauling logs. The skiers kept to the stretch of snow along the side. The road dipped sharply to a stream and they ran straight up-hill. Through the woods they could see a long, low-eaved, weather-beaten building. Through the trees it was a faded yellow. Closer the window frames were painted green. The paint was peeling. Nick knocked his clamps loose with one of his ski sticks and kicked off the skis.

'We might as well carry them up there,' he said.

He climbed the steep road with the skis on his shoulder, kicking his heel nails into the icy footing. He heard George breathing and kicking in his heels just behind him. They stacked the skis against the side of the inn and slapped the snow off each other's trousers, stamped their boots clean, and went in.

Inside it was quite dark. A big porcelain stove shone in the corner of the room. There was a low ceiling. Smooth benches back of dark, wine-stained tables were along each side of the rooms. Two Swiss sat over their pipes and two decies of cloudy new wine next to the stove. The boys took off their jackets and sat against the wall on the other side of the stove. A voice in the next room stopped singing and a girl in a blue apron came in through the door to see what they wanted to drink.

'A bottle of Sion,' Nick said. 'Is that all right, Gidge?'

'Sure,' said George. 'You know more about wine than I do. I like any of it.'

The girl went out.

'There's nothing really can touch skiing, is there?' Nick said. 'The way it feels when you first drop off on a long run.'

'Huh,' said George. 'It's too swell to talk about.'

The girl brought the wine in and they had trouble with the cork. Nick finally opened it. The girl went out and they heard her singing in German in the next room.

'Those specks of cork in it don't matter,' said Nick.

'I wonder if she's got any cake.'

'Let's find out.'

The girl came in and Nick noticed that her apron covered swellingly her pregnancy. I wonder why I didn't see that when she first came in, he thought.

'What were you singing?' he asked her.

'Opera, German opera.' She did not care to discuss the subject. 'We have some apple strudel if you want it.'

'She isn't too cordial, is she?' said George.

'Oh, well. She doesn't know us and she thought we were going to kid her about her singing, maybe. She's from up where they speak German probably and she's touchy about being here, and then she's got that baby coming without being married and she's touchy.'

'How do you know she isn't married?'

'No ring. Hell, no girls get married around here till they're knocked up.'

The door came open and a gang of woodcutters from up the road came in, stamping their boots and steaming in the room. The waitress brought in three litres of new wine for the gang and they sat at the two tables, smoking and quiet, with their hats off, leaning back against the wall or forward on the table. Outside the horses on the wood sledges made an occasional sharp jangle of bells as they tossed their heads.

George and Nick were happy. They were fond of each other. They knew they had the run back home ahead of them.

'When have you got to go back to school?' Nick asked.

'Tonight,' George said. 'I've got to get the ten-forty from Montreux.'

'I wish you could stick over and we could do the Dent du Lys tomorrow.'

'I got to get education,' George said. 'Gee, Mike, don't you wish we could just bum together? Take our skis and go on the train to where there was good running and then go on and put up at pubs and go right across the Oberland and up the Valais and all through the Engadine and just take repair kit and extra sweaters and pyjamas in our rucksacks and not give a damn about school or anything.'

'Yes, and go through the Schwarzwald that way. Gee, the swell places.'

'That's where you went fishing last summer, isn't it?'

'Yes.'

They ate the strudel and drank the rest of the wine.

George leaned back against the wall and shut his eyes.

'Wine always makes me feel this way,' he said.

'Feel bad?' Nick asked.

'No. I feel good, but funny.'

'I know,' Nick said.

'Sure,' said George.

'Should we have another bottle?' Nick asked.

'Not for me,' said George.

They sat there, Nick leaning his elbows on the table, George slumped back against the wall.

'Is Helen going to have a baby?' George said, coming down to the table from the wall.

'Yes.'

'When?'

'Late next summer.'

'Are you glad?'

'Yes, Now.'

'Will you go back to the States?'

'I guess so.'

'Do you want to?'

'No.'

'Does Helen?'

'No.'

George sat silent. He looked at the empty bottle and the empty glasses.

'It's hell isn't it?' he said.

'No. Not exactly,' Nick said.

'Why not?'

'I don't know,' Nick said.

'Will you ever go skiing together in the States?' George said.

'I don't know,' said Nick.

'The mountains aren't much,' George said.

'No,' said Nick. 'They're too rocky. There's too much timber and they're too far away.'

'Yes,' said George, 'that's the way it is in California.'

'Yes,' Nick said, 'that's the way it is everywhere I've ever been.'

'Yes,' said George, 'that's the way it is.'

The Swiss got up and paid and went out.

'I wish we were Swiss,' George said.

'They've all got goitre,' said Nick.

'I don't believe that,' George said.

'Neither do I,' said Nick.

They laughed.

'Maybe we'll never go skiing again, Nick,' George said.

'We've got to,' said Nick. 'It isn't worth while if you can't.'

'We'll go, all right,' George said.

'We've got to,' Nick agreed.

'I wish we could make a promise about it,' George said.

Nick stood up. He buckled his wind jacket tight. He leaned over George and picked up the two ski poles from against the wall. He stuck one of the ski poles into the floor.

'There isn't any good in promising,' he said.

They opened the door and went out. It was very cold. The snow had crusted hard. The road ran up the hill into the pine trees.

They took down their skis from where they leaned against the wall of the inn. Nick put on his gloves. George was already started up the road, his skis on his shoulder. Now they would have the run home together.

My Old Man

I heard the drums coming down the street and then the fifes and the pipes and then they came around the corner, all dancing. The street was full of them. Maera saw him and then I saw him. When they stopped the music for the crouch he hunched down in the street with them all and when they started it again he jumped up and went dancing down the street with them. He was drunk all right.

'You go down after him,' said Maera, 'he hates me.'

So I went down and caught up with them and grabbed him while he was crouched down waiting for the music to break loose and said, 'Come on, Luis. For Christ sake you've got bulls this afternoon.' He didn't listen to me, he was listening so hard for the music to start.

I said, 'Don't be a damn fool, Luis. Come on back to the hotel.'

Then the music started up again and he jumped up and twisted away from me and started dancing. I grabbed his arm and he pulled loose and said, 'Oh leave me alone. You're not my father.'

I went back to the hotel and Maera was on the balcony looking out to see if I'd be bringing him back. He went inside when he saw me and came downstairs disgusted.

'Well,' I said, 'after all he's just an ignorant Mexican savage.'

'Yes,' Maera said, 'and who will kill his bulls after he gets a cornada?'

'We, I suppose,' I said.

'Yes, we,' said Maera. 'We kill the savages' bulls, and the drunkards' bulls, and the riau-riau *dancers' bulls. We kill them. We kill them all right. Yes. Yes. Yes.'*

102

I guess looking at it, now, my old man was cut out for a fat guy, one of those regular little roly fat guys you see around, but he sure never got that way, except a little toward the last, and then it wasn't his fault, he was riding over the jumps only and he could afford to carry plenty of weight then. I remember the way he'd pull on a rubber shirt over a couple of jerseys and a big sweat shirt over that, and get me to run with him in the forenoon in the hot sun. He'd have, maybe, taken a trial trip with one of Razzo's skins early in the morning after just getting in from Torino at four o'clock in the morning and beating it out to the stables in a cab and then with the dew all over everything and the sun just starting to get going, I'd help him pull off his boots and he'd get into a pair of sneakers and all these sweaters and we'd start out.

'Come on, kid,' he'd say, stepping up and down on his toes in front of the jocks' dressing-room, 'let's get moving.'

Then we'd start off jogging around the infield once, maybe with him ahead, running nice, and then turn out the gate and along one of those roads with all the trees along the sides of them that run out from San Siro. I'd go ahead of him when we hit the road and I could run pretty good and I'd look around and he'd be jogging easy just behind me and after a little while I'd look around again and he'd begun to sweat. Sweating heavy and he'd just be dogging it along with his eyes on my back, but when he'd catch me looking at him he'd grin and say, 'Sweating plenty?' When my old man grinned, nobody could help but grin too. We'd keep right on running out toward the mountains and then my old man would yell, 'Hey, Joe!' and I'd look back and he'd be sitting under a tree with a towel he'd had wrapped around his waist wrapped around his neck.

I'd come back and sit down beside him and he'd pull a rope out of his pocket and start skipping rope out in the sun with the sweat pouring off his face and him skipping rope out in the white dust with the rope going cloppety, cloppety, clop, clop, clop, and the sun hotter, and him working hard up and down a patch of the road. Say, it was a treat to see my old man skip rope, too. He could whirr it fast or lop it slow and fancy. Say, you ought to have seen wops look at us sometimes, when they'd come by, going into town walking along with big white steers hauling the cart. They sure looked as though they thought the old man was nuts. He'd start the rope whirring till they'd stop dead still and watch him, then give the steers a cluck and a poke with the goad and get going again.

When I'd sit watching him working out in the hot sun I sure felt fond of him. He sure was fun and he done his work so hard and he'd finish up with a regular whirring that'd drive the sweat out on his face like water and then sling the rope at the tree and come over and sit down with me and lean back against the tree with the towel and a sweater wrapped around his neck.

'Sure it's hell keeping it down, Joe,' he'd say, and lean back and shut his eyes and breathe long and deep, 'it ain't like when you're a kid.' Then he'd get up and before he started to cool we'd jog along back to the stables. That's the way it was keeping down to weight. He was worried all the time. Most jocks can just about ride off all they want to. A jock loses about a kilo every time he rides, but my old man was sort of dried out and he couldn't keep down his kilos without all that running.

I remember once at San Siro, Regoli, a little wop, that was riding for Buzoni, came out across the paddock going to the bar for something cool; and flicking his boots with his whip, after he'd just weighed in and my old man had just weighed in too, and came out with the saddle under his arm looking red-faced and tired and too big for his silks and he stood there looking at young Regoli standing up to the outdoors bar, cool and kid-looking, and I said, 'What's the matter, Dad?' 'cause I thought maybe Regoli had bumped him or something and he just looked at Regoli and said, 'Oh, to hell with it,' and went on to the dressing-room.

Well, it would have been all right, maybe, if we'd stayed in Milan and ridden at Milan and Torino, 'cause if there ever were any easy courses, it's those two. 'Pianola Joe,' my old man said when he dismounted in the winning stall after what the wops thought was a hell of a steeplechase. I asked him once. 'This course rides itself. It's the pace you're going at that makes riding the jumps dangerous, Joe. We ain't going any pace here, and they ain't really bad jumps either. But it's the pace always – not the jumps – that makes the trouble.'

San Siro was the swellest course I'd ever seen but the old man said it was a dog's life. Going back and forth between Mirafiore and San Siro and riding just about every day in the week with a train ride every other night.

I was nuts about the horses, too. There's something about it, when they come out and go up the track to the post. Sort of dancy and tight looking with the jock keeping a tight hold on them and maybe easing off a little and letting them run a little going up. Then once they were at the barrier it got me worse than anything. Especially at San Siro with that big green infield and the mountains way off and the fat wop starter with his big whip and the jocks fiddling them around and then the barrier snapping up and that bell going off and them all getting off in a bunch and then commencing to string out. You know the way a bunch of skins gets off. If you're up in the stand with a pair of glasses all you see is them plunging off and then that bell goes off and it seems like it rings for a thousand years and then they come sweeping round the turn. There wasn't ever anything like it for me.

But my old man said one day, in the dressing-room, when he was getting into his street clothes, 'None of these things are horses, Joe. They'd kill that bunch of skates for their hides and hoofs up at Paris.' That was the day he'd won the Premio Commercio with Lantorna shooting her out of the field the last hundred metres like pulling a cork out of a bottle.

It was right after the Premio Commercio that we pulled out and left Italy. My old man and Holbrook and a fat wop in a straw hat that kept wiping his face with a handkerchief were having an argument at a table in the Galleria. They were all talking French and the two of them was after my old man about something. Finally he didn't say anything any more but just sat there and looked at Holbrook, and the two of them kept after him, first one talking and then the other, and the fat wop always butting in on Holbrook.

'You go out and buy me a *Sportsman*, will you, Joe?' my old man said, and handed me a couple of Soldi without looking away from Holbrook.

So I went out of the Galleria and walked over to in front of the Scala and bought a paper, and came back and stood a little way away because I didn't want to butt in and my old man was sitting back in his chair looking down at his coffee and fooling with a spoon and Holbrook and the big wop were standing and the big wop was wiping his face and shaking his head. And I came up and my old man acted just as though the two of them weren't standing there and said, 'Want an ice, Joe?' Holbrook looked down at my old man and said slow and careful, 'You son of a bitch,' and he and the fat wop went out through the stables.

My old man sat there and sort of smiled at me, but his face was white and he looked sick as hell and I was scared and felt sick inside because I knew something had happened and I didn't see how anybody could call my old man a son of a bitch, and get away with it. My old man opened up the *Sportsman* and studied the handicaps for a while, and then he said, 'You got to take a lot of things in this world, Joe.' And three days later we left Milan for good on the Turin train for Paris, after an auction sale out in front of Turner's stables of everything we couldn't get into a trunk and a suitcase.

We got into Paris early in the morning in a long, dirty station the old man told me was the Gare de Lyon. Paris was an awful big town after Milan. Seems like in Milan everybody is going somewhere and all the trams run somewhere and there ain't any sort of mix-up, but Paris is all balled up and they never do straighten it out. I got to like it, though, part of it, anyway, and say, it's got the best race courses in the world. Seems as though that were the thing that keeps it all going about the only thing you can figure on is that every day the buses will be going out to whatever track they're running at, going right out through everything to the track. I never really got to know Paris well, because I just came in about once or twice a week with the old man from Maisons and he always sat at the Café de la Paix on the Opéra side with the rest of the gang from Maisons and I guess that's one of the busiest parts of town. But, say, it is funny that a big town like Paris wouldn't have a Galleria, isn't it?

Well, we went out to live at Maisons-Lafitte, where just about everybody lives except the gang at Chantilly, with a Mrs Meyers that runs a boarding-house. Maisons is about the swellest place to live I've ever seen in all my life. The town ain't so much, but there's a lake and a swell forest that we used to go bumming in all day, a couple of us kids, and my old man made me a sling shot and we got a lot of things with it but the best one was a magpie. Young Dick Atkinson shot a rabbit with it one day and we put it under a tree and were all sitting around and Dick had some cigarettes and all of a sudden the rabbit jumped up and beat it into the brush and we chased it but we couldn't find it. Gee, we had fun at Maisons. Mrs Meyers used to give me lunch in the morning, and I'd be gone all day. I learned to talk French quick. It's an easy language.

As soon as we got to Maisons, my old man wrote to Milan for his licence and he was pretty worried till it came. He used to sit around the Café de Paris in Maisons with the gang, there were lots of guys he'd known when he rode up at Paris, before the war, lived at Maisons, and there's a lot of time to sit around because the work around a racing stable, for the jocks, that is, is all cleaned up by nine o'clock in the morning. They take the first bunch of skins out to gallop at 5.30 in the morning and they work the second lot at 8 o'clock. That means getting up early all right and going to bed early, too. If a jock's riding for somebody too, he can't go boozing around because the trainer always has an eye on him if he's a kid and if he ain't a kid he's always got an eye on himself. So mostly if a jock ain't working he sits around the Café de Paris with the gang and they can all sit around about two or three hours in front of some drink like vermouth and seltz and they talk and tell stories and shoot pool and it's sort of like a club or the Galleria in Milan. Only it ain't really like the Galleria because there everybody is going by all the time and there's everybody around at the tables.

Well, my old man got his licence all right. They sent it through to him without a word and he rode a couple of times. Amiens, up country and that sort of thing, but he didn't seem to get any engagement. Everybody liked him and whenever I'd come into the Café in the forenoon I'd find somebody drinking with him because my old man wasn't tight like most of these jockeys that have got the first dollar they made riding at the World's Fair in St Louis in nineteen nought four. That's what my old man would say when he'd kid George Burns. But it seemed like everybody steered clear of giving my old man any mounts.

We went out to wherever they were running every day with the car from Maisons and that was the most fun of all. I was glad when the horses came back from Deauville and the summer. Even though it meant no more bumming in the woods, 'cause then we'd ride to Enghien or Tremblay or St Cloud and watch them from the trainers' and jockeys' stand. I sure learned about racing from going out with that gang and the fun of it was going every day.

I remember once out at St Cloud. It was a big two-hundred-thousand-franc race with seven entries and War Cloud a big favourite. I went around to the paddock to see the horses with my old man and you never saw such horses. This War Cloud is a great big yellow horse that looks just like nothing but run. I never saw such a horse. He was being led around the paddocks with his head down and when he went by me I felt all hollow inside he was so beautiful. There never was such a wonderful, lean, running-built horse. And he went around the paddock putting his feet just so and quiet and careful and moving easy like he knew just what he had to do and not jerking and standing up on his legs and getting wild-eyed like you see these selling platers with a shot of dope in them. The crowd was so thick I couldn't see him again except just his legs going by and some yellow and my old man started out through the crowd and I followed him over to the jocks' dressing-room back in the trees and there was a big crowd around there, too, but the man at the door in a derby nodded to my old man and we got in and everybody was sitting around and getting dressed and pulling shirts over their heads and pulling boots on and it all smelled hot and sweaty and linimenty and outside it was the crowd looking in.

The old man went over and sat down beside George Gardner that was getting into his pants and said, 'What's the dope, George?' just in an ordinary tone of voice, 'cause there ain't any use him feeling around because George either can tell him or he can't tell him.

'He won't win,' George says very low, leaning over and buttoning the bottoms of his breeches.

'Who will?' my old man says, leaning over close so nobody can hear.

'Foxless,' George says, 'and if he does, save me a couple of tickets.'

My old man says something in a regular voice to George and George says, 'Don't ever bet on anything I tell you,' kidding like, and we beat it out and through all the crowd that was looking in, over to the 100-franc mutuel machine. But I knew something big was up because George is War Cloud's jockey. On the way he gets one of the yellow odds-sheets with the starting-prices on and War Cloud is only paying 5 for 10, Cefisidote is next at 3 to 1 and fifth down the list this Foxless at 8 to 1. My old man bets five thousand on Foxless to win and puts on a thousand to place and we went around back of the grandstand to go up the stairs and get a place to watch the race.

We were jammed up tight and first a man in a long coat with a grey tall hat and a whip folded up in his hand came out and then one after another the horses, with the jocks up and a stable boy holding the bridle on each side and walking along, followed the old guy. That big yellow horse War Cloud came first. He didn't look so big when you first looked at him until you saw the length of his legs and the whole way he's built and the way he moves. Gosh, I never saw such a horse. George Gardner was riding him and they moved along slow, back of the old guy in the grey tall hat that walked along like he was a ring master in a circus. Back of War Cloud, moving along smooth and yellow in the sun, was a good looking black with a nice head with Tommy Archibald riding him; and after the black was a string of five more horses all moving along slow in a procession past the grandstand and the pesage. My old man said the black was Foxless and I took a good look at him and he was a nice-looking horse, all right, but nothing like War Cloud.

Everybody cheered War Cloud when he went by and he sure was one swell-looking horse. The procession of them went around on the other side past the pelouse and then back up to the near end of the course and the circus master had the stable boys turn them loose one after another so they could gallop by the stands on their way up to the post and let everybody have a good look at them. They weren't at the post hardly any time at all when the gong started and you could see them way off across the infield all in a bunch starting on the first swing like a lot of little toy horses. I was watching them through the glasses and War Cloud was running well back, with one of the bays making the pace. They swept down and around and came pounding past and War Cloud was way back when they passed us and this Foxless horse in front and going smooth. Gee, it's awful when they go by you and then you have to watch them go farther away and get smaller and smaller and then all bunched up on the turns and then come around towards into the stretch and you feel like swearing and god-damning worse and worse. Finally they made the last turn and came into the straightaway with this Foxless horse way out in front. Everybody was looking funny and saying 'War Cloud' in a sort of sick way and them pounding nearer down the stretch, and then something came out of the pack right into my glasses like a horse-headed yellow streak and everybody began to yell 'War Cloud' as though they were crazy. War Cloud came on faster than I'd ever seen anything in my life and pulled up on Foxless that was going fast as any black horse could go with the jock flogging hell out of him with the gad and they were right dead neck and neck for a second but War Cloud seemed going about twice as fast with those great jumps and that head out – but it was while they were neck and neck that they passed the winning-post and when the numbers went up in the slots the first one was 2 and that meant that Foxless had won.

I felt all trembly and funny inside and then we were jammed in with the people going downstairs to stand in front of the board where they'd post what Foxless paid. Honest, watching the race I'd forgot how much my old man had bet on Foxless. I'd wanted War Cloud to win so damned bad. But now it was all over it was swell to know we had the winner.

'Wasn't it a swell race, Dad?' I said to him.

He looked at me sort of funny with his derby hat on the back of his head. 'George Gardner's a swell jockey all right,' he said. 'It sure took a great jock to keep that War Cloud horse from winning.'

Of course I knew it was funny all the time. But my old man

saying that right out like that sure took the kick all out of it for me and I didn't get the real kick back again ever, even when they posted the numbers upon the board and the bell rang to pay off and we saw that Foxless paid 67.50 for 10. All round people were saying, 'Poor War Cloud! Poor War Cloud!' And I thought, I wish I were a jockey and could have rode him instead of that son of a bitch because I'd always liked him and besides he'd given us the winner, but I guess that's what he is, all right.

My old man had a big lot of money after that race and he took to coming into Paris oftener. If they raced at Tremblay he'd have them drop him in town on their way back to Maisons and he and I'd sit out in front of the Café de la Paix and watch the people go by. It's funny sitting there. There's streams of people going by and all sorts of guys come up and want to sell you things, and I loved to sit there with my old man. That was when we'd have the most fun. Guys would come by selling funny rabbits that jumped if you squeezed a bulb and they'd come up to us and my old man would kid them. He could talk French just like English and all those kind of guys knew him 'cause you can always tell a jockey – and then we always sat at the same table and they got used to seeing us there. There were guys selling matrimonial papers and girls selling rubber eggs that when you squeezed them a rooster came out of them and one old wormy-looking guy that went by with postcards of Paris, showing them to everybody, and, of course, nobody ever bought any, and then he would come back and show the under side of the pack and they would all be smutty postcards and lots of people would dig down and buy them.

Gee, I remember the funny people that used to go by. Girls around supper time looking for somebody to take them out to eat and they'd speak to my old man and he'd make some joke at them in French and they'd pat me on the head and go on. Once there was an American woman sitting with her kid daughter at the next table to us and they were both eating ices and I smiled at her and she smiled at me but that was all that ever come of it because I looked for her mother and her every day and I made up ways that I was going to speak to her and I wondered if I got to know her if her mother would let me take her out to Auteuil or Tremblay but I never saw either of them again. Anyway, I guess it wouldn't have been any good, anyway, because looking back on it I remember the way I thought out would be best to speak to her was to say, 'Pardon me, but perhaps I can give you a winner at Enghien today?' And, after all, maybe she would have thought I was a tout instead of really trying to give her a winner.

We'd sit at the Café de la Paix, my old man and me, and we had a big drag with the waiter because my old man drank whisky and it cost five francs, and that meant a good tip when the saucers were counted up. My old man was drinking more than I've ever seen him, but he wasn't riding at all now and besides he said that whisky kept his weight down. But I noticed he was putting it on, all right, just the same. He'd busted away from his old gang out at Maisons and seemed to like just sitting around the boulevard with me. But he was dropping money every day at the track. He'd feel sort of doleful after the last race, if he'd lost on the day, until we'd get to our table and he'd have his first whisky and then he'd be fine.

He'd be reading the *Paris-Sport* and he'd look over at me and say, 'Where's your girl, Joe?' to kid me on account I had told him about the girl that day at the next table. And I'd get red, but I liked being kidded about her. It gave me a good feeling. 'Keep your eye peeled for her, Joe,' he'd say, 'she'll be back.'

He'd ask me questions about things and some of the things I'd say he'd laugh. And then he'd get started talking about things. About riding down in Egypt, or at St Moritz on the ice before my mother died, and about during the war when they had regular races down in the south of France without any purses, or betting or crowds or anything just to keep the breed up. Regular races with the jocks riding hell out of the horses. Gee, I could listen to my old man talk by the hour, especially when he'd had a couple or so of drinks. He'd tell me about when he was a boy in Kentucky and going coon hunting, and the old days in the States before everything went on the bum there. And he'd say, 'Joe, when we've got a decent stake, you're going back there to the States and go to school.'

'What've I got to go back there to go to school for when

everything's on the bum there?' I'd ask him.

'That's different,' he'd say and get the waiter over and pay the pile of saucers and we'd get a taxi to the Gare St Lazare and get on the train out to Maisons.

One day at Auteuil after a selling steeplechase, my old man bought in the winner for 30,000 francs. He had to bid a little to get him but the stable let the horse go finally and my old man had his permit and his colours in a week. Gee, I felt proud when my old man was an owner. He fixed it up for stable space with Charles Drake and cut out coming in to Paris, and started his running and sweating out again, and him and I were the whole stable gang. Our horse's name was Gilford, he was Irish bred and a nice, sweet jumper. My old man figured that training him and riding him, himself, he was a good investment. I was proud of everything and I thought Gilford was as good a horse as War Cloud. He was a good, solid jumper, a bay, with plenty of speed on the flat, if you asked him for it, and he was a nice-looking horse, too.

Gee, I was fond of him. The first time he started with my old man up, he finished third in a 2,500-metre hurdle race and when my old man got off him, all sweating and happy in the place stall, and went in to weigh, I felt as proud of him as though it was the first race he'd ever placed in. You see, when a guy ain't been riding for a long time, you can't make yourself really believe that he has ever rode. The whole thing was different now, 'cause down in Milan, even big races never seemed to make any difference to my old man, if he won he wasn't ever excited or anything, and now it was so I couldn't hardly sleep the night before a race and I knew my old man was excited too, even if he didn't show it. Riding for yourself makes an awful difference.

Second time Gilford and my old man started, was a rainy Sunday at Auteuil, in the Prix du Marat, a 4,500-metre steeplechase. As soon as he'd gone out I beat it up in the stand with the new glasses my old man had bought for me to watch them. They started way over at the far end of the course and there was some trouble at the barrier. Something with goggle blinders on was making a great fuss and rearing around and busted the barrier once, but I could see my old man in our black jacket, with a white cross and a black cap, sitting up on Gilford, and patting him with his hand. Then they were going off in a jump and out of sight behind the trees and the gong going for dear life and the pari-mutuel wickets rattling down. Gosh, I was so excited, I was afraid to look at them, but I fixed the glasses on the place where they would come out back of the trees and then out they came with the old black jacket going third and they all sailing over the jump like birds. Then they went out of sight again and then they came pounding out and down the hill and all going nice and sweet and easy and taking the fence smooth in a bunch, and moving away from us all solid. Looked as though you could walk across their backs they were all so bunched and going so smooth. Then they bellied over the big double Bullfinch and something came down. I couldn't see who it was, but in a minute the horse was up and galloping free and the field, all bunched still, sweeping around the long left turn into the straightaway. They jumped the stone wall and came jammed down the stretch toward the big water-jump right in front of the stands. I saw them coming and hollered at my old man as he went by, and he was leading by about a length and riding way out, and light as a monkey, and they were racing for the water-jump. They took off over the big hedge of the water-jump in a pack and then there was a crash, and two horses pulled sideways out of it, and kept on going, and three others were piled up. I couldn't see my old man anywhere. One horse kneed himself up and the jock had hold of the bridle and mounted and went slamming on after the place money. The other horse was up and away by himself, jerking his head and galloping with the bridle rein hanging and the jock staggered over to one side of the track against the fence. Then Gilford rolled over to one side off my old man and got up and started to run on three legs with his front off hoof dangling and there was my old man laying there on the grass flat out with his face up and blood all over the side of his head. I ran down the stand and bumped into a jam of people and got to the rail and a cop grabbed me and held me and two big stretcher-bearers were going out after my old man and around on the other side of the course I saw three horses strung way out, coming out of the trees and taking the jump.

114

My old man was dead when they brought him in and while a doctor was listening to his heart with a thing plugged in his ear, I heard a shot up the track that mean they'd killed Gilford. I lay down beside my old man, when they carried the stretcher into the hospital room, and hung on to the stretcher and cried and cried, and he looked so white and gone and so awfully dead, and I couldn't help feeling that if my old man was dead maybe they didn't need to have shot Gilford. His hoof might have got well. I don't know. I loved my old man so much.

Then a couple of guys came in and one of them patted me on the back and then went over and looked at my old man and then pulled a sheet off the cot and spread it over him; and the other was telephoning in French for them to send the ambulance to take him out to Maisons. And I couldn't stop crying, crying and choking, sort of, and George Gardner came in and sat down beside me on the floor and put his arm around me and says, 'Come on, Joe, old boy. Get up and we'll go out and wait for the ambulance.'

George and I went out to the gate and I was trying to stop bawling and George wiped off my face with his handkerchief and we were standing back a little ways while the crowd was going out of the gate and a couple of guys stopped near us while we were waiting for the crowd to get through the gate and one of them was counting a bunch of mutuel tickets and he said, 'Well, Butler got his, all right.'

The other guy said, 'I don't give a good goddam if he did, the crook. He had it coming to him on the stuff he's pulled.'

'I'll say he had,' said the other guy, and tore the bunch of tickets in two.

And George Gardner looked at me to see if I'd heard and I had all right, and he said, 'Don't you listen to what those bums said, Joe. Your old man was one swell guy.'

But I don't know. Seems like when they get started they don't leave a guy nothing.

Big Two-Hearted River: Part I

Maera lay still his head on his arms, his face in the sand. He felt warm and sticky from the bleeding. Each time he felt the horn coming. Sometimes the bull only bumped him with his head. Once the horn went all way through him and he felt it go into the sand. Someone had the bull by the tail. They were swearing at him and flopping the cape in his face. Then the bull was gone. Some men picked Maera up and started to run with him toward the barriers through the gate out the passageway around under the grandstand to the infirmary. They laid Maera down on a cot and one of the men went out for the doctor. The others stood around. The doctor came running from the corral where he had been sewing up picador horses. He had to stop and wash his hands. There was a great shouting going on in the grandstand overhead. Maera felt everything getting larger and larger and then smaller and smaller. Then it got larger and larger and then smaller and smaller. Then everything commenced to run faster and faster as when they speed up on a cinematograph film. Then he was dead.

The train went on up the track out of sight, around one of the hills of burnt timber. Nick sat down on the bundle of canvas and bedding the baggage men had pitched out of the door of the baggage car. There was no town, nothing but the rails and the burned-over country. The thirteen saloons that had lined the one street of Seney had not left a trace. The foundations of the Mansion House hotel stuck up above the ground. The stone was chipped and split by the fire. It was all that was left

116

of the town of Seney. Even the surface had been burned off the ground.

Nick looked at the burned-over stretch of hillside, where he had expected to find the scattered houses of the town and then walked down the railroad track to the bridge over the river. The river was there. It swirled against the log piles of the bridge. Nick looked down into the clear, brown water, coloured from the pebbly bottom, and watched the trout keeping themselves steady in the current with wavering fins. As he watched them they changed their positions by quick angles, only to hold steady in the fast water again. Nick watched them a long time.

He watched them holding themselves with their noses into the current, many trout in deep, fast-moving water, slightly distorted as he watched far down through the glassy convex surface of the pool, its surface pushing and swelling smooth against the resistance of the log-driven piles of the bridge. At the bottom of the pool were the big trout. Nick did not see them at first. Then he saw them at the bottom of the pool, big trout looking to hold themselves on the gravel bottom in a varying mist of gravel and sand, raised in spurts by the current.

Nick looked down into the pool from the bridge. It was a hot day. A kingfisher flew up the stream. It was a long time since Nick had looked into a stream and seen trout. They were very satisfactory. As the shadow of the kingfisher moved up the stream, a big trout shot upstream in a long angle, only his shadow marking the angle, then lost his shadow as he came through the surface of the water, caught the sun, and then, as he went back into the stream under the surface, his shadow seemed to float down the stream with the current, unresisting, to his post under the bridge where he tightened facing up into the current.

Nick's heart tightened as the trout moved. He felt all the old feeling.

He turned and looked down the stream. It stretched away, pebbly-bottomed with shallows and big boulders and a deep pool as it curved away around the foot of a bluff.

Nick walked back up the ties to where his pack lay in the cinders beside the railway track. He was happy. He adjusted the pack harness around the bundle, pulling straps tight, slung the pack on his back, got his arms through the shoulder straps and took some of the pull off his shoulders by leaning his forehead against the wide bank of the tump-line. Still, it was too heavy. It was much too heavy. He had his leather rod-case in his hand and leaning forward to keep the weight of the pack high on his shoulders he walked along the road that paralleled the railway track, leaving the burned town behind in the heat, and then turned off around a hill with a high, fire-scarred hill on either side on to a road that went back into the country. He walked along the road feeling the ache from the pull of the heavy pack. The road climbed steadily. It was hard work walking up-hill. His muscles ached and the day was hot, but Nick felt happy. He felt he had left everything behind, the need for thinking, the need to write, other needs. It was all back of him.

From the time he had gotten down off the train and the baggage man had thrown his pack out of the open car door things had been different. Seney was burned, the country was burned over and changed, but it did not matter. It could not all be burned. He knew that. He hiked along the road, sweating in the sun, climbing to cross the range of hills that separated the railway from the pine plains.

The road ran on, dipping occasionally, but always climbing, Nick went on up. Finally the road after going parallel to the burnt hillside reached the top. Nick leaned back against a stump and slipped out of the pack harness. Ahead of him, as far as he could see, was the pine plain. The burned country stopped off at the left with the range of hills. On ahead islands of dark pine trees rose out of the plain. Far off to the left was the line of the river. Nick followed it with his eye and caught glints of the water in the sun.

There was nothing but the pine plain ahead of him, until the far blue hills that marked the Lake Superior height of land. He could hardly see them, faint and far away in the heat-light over the plain. If he looked too steadily they were gone. But if he only half-looked they were there, the far-off hills of the height of land.

Nick sat down against the charred stump and smoked a

cigarette. His pack balanced on top of the stump, harness holding ready, a hollow moulded in it from his pack. Nick sat smoking, looking out over the country. He did not need to get his map out. He knew where he was from the position of the river.

As he smoked, his legs stretched out in front of him, he noticed a grasshopper walk along the ground and up on to his woollen sock. The grasshopper was black. As he had walked along the road, climbing, he had started many grasshoppers from the dust. They were all black. They were not the big grasshoppers with yellow and black or red and black wings whirring out from their black wing sheathing as they fly up. These were just ordinary hoppers, but all a sooty black in colour. Nick had wondered about them as he walked, without really thinking about them. Now, as he watched the black hopper that was nibbling at the wool of his sock with its four-way lip, he realized that they had all turned black from living in the burned-over land. He realized that the fire must have come the year before, but the grasshoppers were all black now. He wondered how long they would stay that way.

Carefully he reached his hand down and took hold of the hopper by the wings. He turned him up, all his legs walking in the air, and looked at his jointed belly. Yes, it was black too, iridescent where the back and head were dusty.

'Go on, hopper,' Nick said, speaking out loud for the first time. 'Fly away somewhere.'

He tossed the grasshopper into the air and watched him sail away to a charcoal stump across the road.

Nick stood up. He leaned his back against the weight of his pack where it rested upright on the stump and got his arms through the shoulder straps. He stood with the pack on his back on the brow of the hill looking out across the country toward the distant river and then struck down the hillside away from the road. Underfoot the ground was good walking. Two hundred yards down the hillside the fire-line stopped. Then it was sweet fern, growing ankle high, to walk through, and clumps of jack pines; a long undulating country with frequent rises and descents, sandy underfoot and the country alive again.

Nick kept his direction by the sun. He knew where he wanted to strike the river and he kept on through the pine plain, mounting small rises to see other rises ahead of him and sometimes from the top of a rise a great solid island of pines off to his right or his left. He broke off some sprigs of the heathery sweet fern, and put them under his pack straps. The chafing crushed it and he smelled it as he walked.

He was tired and very hot, walking across the uneven, shadeless pine plain. At any time he knew he would strike the river by turning off to his left. It could not be more than a mile away. But he kept on toward the north to hit the river as far upstream as he could go in one day's walking.

For some time as he walked Nick had been in sight of one of the big islands of pine standing out above the rolling high ground he was crossing. He dipped down and then as he came slowly up to the crest of the ridge he turned and made toward the pine trees.

There was no underbrush in the island pine trees. The trunks of the trees went straight up or slanted toward each other. The trunks were straight and brown without branches. The branches were high above. Some interlocked to make a solid shadow on the brown forest floor. Around the grove of trees was a bare space. It was brown and soft underfoot as Nick walked on it. This was the over-lapping of the pine needle floor, extending out beyond the width of the high branches. The trees had grown tall and the branches moved high, leaving the sun this bare space they had once covered with shadow. Sharp at the edge of this extension of the forest floor commenced the sweet fern.

Nick slipped off his pack and lay down in the shade. He lay on his back and looked up into the pine trees. His neck and back and the small of his back rested as he stretched. The earth felt good against his back. He looked up at the sky, through the branches, and then shut his eyes. He opened them and looked up again. There was a wind high up in the branches. He shut his eyes again and went to sleep.

Nick woke stiff and cramped. The sun was nearly down. His pack was heavy and the straps painful as he lifted it on. He leaned over with the pack on and picked up the leather rod-case and started out from the pine trees across the sweet fern swale, toward the river. He knew it could not be more than a mile.

He came down a hillside covered with stumps into a meadow. At the edge of the meadow flowed the river. Nick was glad to get to the river. He walked upstream through the meadow. His trousers were soaked with the dew as he walked. After the hot day, the dew had come quickly and heavily. The river made no sound. It was too fast and smooth. At the edge of the meadow, before he mounted to a piece of high ground to make camp, Nick looked down the river at the trout rising. They were rising to insects come from the swamp on the other side of the stream when the sun went down. The trout jumped out of water to take them. While Nick walked through the little stretch of meadow alongside the stream, trout had jumped high out of water. Now as he looked down the river, the insects must be settling on the surface, for the trout were feeding steadily all down the stream. As far down the long stretch as he could see, the trout were rising, making circles all down the surface of the water, as though it were starting to rain.

The ground rose, wooded and sandy, to overlook the meadow, the stretch of river and the swamp. Nick dropped his pack and rod-case and looked for a level piece of ground. He was very hungry and he wanted to make his camp before he cooked. Between two jack-pines, the ground was quite level. He took the axe out of the pack and chopped out two projecting roots. That levelled a piece of ground large enough to sleep on. He smoothed out the sandy soil with his hand and pulled all the sweet fern bushes by their roots. His hands smelled good from the sweet fern. He smoothed the uprooted earth. He did not want anything making lumps under the blankets. One he folded double, next to the ground. The other two he spread on top.

With the axe he slit off a bright slab of pine from one of the stumps and split it into pegs for the tent. He wanted them long and solid to hold in the ground. With the tent unpacked and spread on the ground, the pack, leaning against a jack-pine, looked much smaller. Nick tied the rope that served the tent for a ridge-pole to the trunk of one of the pine trees and pulled the tent up off the ground with the other end of the rope and

121

tied it to the other pine. The tent hung on the rope like a canvas blanket on a clothes-line. Nick poked a pole he had cut up under the back peak of the canvas and then made it a tent by pegging out the sides. He pegged the sides out taut and drove the pegs deep, hitting them down into the ground with the flat of the axe until the rope loops were buried and the canvas was drum tight.

Across the mouth of the tent Nick fixed cheesecloth to keep out mosquitoes. He crawled inside under the mosquito bar with various things from the pack to put at the head of the bed under the slant of the canvas. Inside the tent the light came through the brown canvas. It smelled pleasantly of canvas. Already there was something mysterious and homelike. Nick was happy as he crawled inside the tent. He had not been unhappy all day. This was different though. Now things were done. There had been this to do. Now it was done. It had been a hard trip. He was very tired. That was done. He had made his camp. He was settled. Nothing could touch him. It was a good place to camp. He was there, in the good place. He was in his home where he had made it. Now he was hungry.

He came out, crawling under the cheesecloth. It was quite dark outside. It was lighter in the tent.

Nick went over to the pack and found, with his fingers, a long nail in a paper sack of nails, in the bottom of the pack. He drove it into the pine tree, holding it close and hitting it gently with the flat of the axe. He hung the pack up on the nail. All his supplies were in the pack. They were off the ground and sheltered now.

Nick was hungry. He did not believe he had ever been hungrier. He opened and emptied a can of pork and beans and a can of spaghetti into the frying pan.

'I've got a right to eat this kind of stuff, if I'm willing to carry it,' Nick said. His voice sounded strange in the darkening woods. He did not speak again.

He started a fire with some chunks of pine he got with the axe from a stump. Over the fire he stuck a wire grill, pushing the four legs down into the ground with his boot. Nick put the frying-pan on the grill over the flames. He was hungrier. The beans and spaghetti warmed. Nick stirred them and mixed them together. They began to bubble, making little bubbles that rose with difficulty to the surface. There was a good smell. Nick got out a bottle of tomato catchup and cut four slices of bread. The little bubbles were coming faster now. Nick sat down beside the fire and lifted the frying-pan off. He poured about half the contents out into a tin plate. It spread slowly on the plate. Nick knew it was too hot. He poured on some tomato catchup. He knew the beans and spaghetti were still too hot. He looked at the fire, then at the tent, he was not going to spoil it all by burning his tongue. For years he had never enjoyed fried bananas because he had never been able to wait for them to cool. His tongue was very sensitive. He was very hungry. Across the river in the swamp, in the almost dark, he saw a mist rising. He looked at the tent once more. All right. He took a full spoonful from the plate.

'Chrise,' Nick said. 'Geezus Chrise,' he said happily.

He ate the whole plateful before he remembered the bread. Nick finished the second plateful with the bread, mopping the plate shiny. He had not eaten since a cup of coffee and a ham sandwich in the station restaurant at St Ignace. It had been a very fine experience. He had been that hungry before, but had not been able to satisfy it. He could have made camp hours before if he had wanted to. There was plenty of good places to camp on the river. But this was good.

Nick tucked two big chips of pine under the grill. The fire flared up. He had forgotten to get water for the coffee. Out of the pack he got a folding canvas bucket and walked down the hill, across the edge of the meadow, to the stream. The other bank was in the white mist. The grass was wet and cold as he knelt on the bank and dipped the canvas bucket into the stream. It bellied and bellied hard in the current. The water was ice cold. Nick rinsed the bucket and carried it full up to the camp. Up away from the stream it was not so cold.

Nick drove another big nail and hung up the bucket full of water. He dipped the coffee-pot half full, put some more chips under the grill on to the fire, and put the pot on. He could not remember which way he had made coffee. He could remember an argument about it with Hopkins, but not which side he had taken. He decided to bring it to a boil. He remembered now that was Hopkins's way. He had once argued about everything with Hopkins. While he waited for the coffee to boil, he opened a small can of apricots. He liked to open cans. He emptied the can of apricots out into a tin cup. While he watched the coffee on the fire, he drank the juice syrup of the apricots, carefully at first to keep from spilling, then meditatively, sucking the apricots down. They were better than fresh apricots.

The coffee boiled as he watched. The lid came up and coffee and grounds ran down the side of the pot. Nick took it off the grill. It was a triumph for Hopkins. He put sugar in the empty apricot cup and poured some of the coffee out to cool. It was too hot to pour and he used his hat to hold the handle of the coffee-pot. He would not let it steep in the pot at all. Not the first cup. It should be straight Hopkins all the way. Hop deserved that. He was a very serious coffee drinker. He was the most serious man Nick had ever known. Not heavy, serious. That was a long time ago. Hopkins spoke without moving his lips. He had played polo. He made millions of dollars in Texas. He had borrowed car fare to go to Chicago, when the wire came that his first big well had come in. He could have wired for money. That would have been too slow. They called Hop's girl the Blonde Venus. Hop did not mind because she was not his real girl. Hopkins said very confidently that none of them would make fun of his real girl. He was right. Hopkins went away when the telegram came. That was on the Black River. It took eight days for the telegram to reach him. Hopkins gave away his .22 calibre Colt automatic pistol to Nick. He gave his camera to Bill. It was to remember him always by. They were all going fishing again next summer. The Hop Head was rich. He would get a yacht and they would all cruise along the north shore of Lake Superior. He was excited but serious. They said good-bye and all felt bad. It broke up the trip. They never saw Hopkins again. That was a long time ago on the Black River.

Nick drank the coffee, the coffee according to Hopkins. The coffee was bitter. Nick laughed. It made a good ending to the story. His mind was starting to work. He knew he could choke it because he was tired enough. He spilled the coffee out of the pot and shook the grounds loose into the fire. He lit a cigarette and went inside the tent. He took off his shoes and trousers, sitting on the blankets, rolled the shoes up inside the trousers for a pillow and got in between the blankets.

Out through the front of the tent he watched the glow of the fire, when the night wind blew on it. It was a quiet night. The swamp was perfectly quiet. Nick stretched under the blanket comfortably. A mosquito hummed close to his ear. Nick sat up and lit a match. The mosquito was on the canvas, over his head. Nick moved the match quickly up to it. The mosquito made a satisfactory hiss in the flame. The match went out. Nick lay down again under the blanket. He turned on his side and shut his eyes. He was sleepy. He felt sleep coming. He curled up under the blanket and went to sleep.

Big Two-Hearted River: Part II

They hanged Sam Cardinella at six o'clock in the morning in the corridor of the county jail. The corridor was high and narrow with tiers of cells on either side. All the cells were occupied. The men had been brought in for the hanging. Five men sentenced to be hanged were in the five top cells. Three of the men to be hanged were Negroes. They were very frightened. One of the white men sat on his cot with his head in his hands. The other lay flat on his cot with a blanket wrapped around his head.

They came out on to the gallows through a door in the wall. There were seven of them including two priests. They were carrying Sam Cardinella. He had been like that since about four o'clock in the morning.

While they were strapping his legs together two guards held him up and the two priests were whispering to him. 'Be a man, my son,' said one priest. When they came toward him with the cap to go over his head Sam Cardinella lost control of his sphincter muscle. The guards who had been holding him up both dropped him. They were both disgusted. 'How about a chair, Will?' asked one of the guards. 'Better get one,' said a man in a derby hat.

When they all stepped back on the scaffolding back of the drop, which was very heavy, built of oak and steel and swung on ball bearings, Sam Cardinella was left sitting there strapped tight, the younger of the two priests kneeling beside the chair. The priest skipped back on to the scaffolding, just before the drop fell.

*

In the morning the sun was up and the tent was starting to get hot. Nick crawled out under the mosquito netting stretched across the mouth of the tent, to look at the morning. The grass was wet on his hands as he came out. He held his trousers and his shoes in his hands. The sun was just up over the hill. There was the meadow, the river, and the swamp. There were birch trees in the green of the swamp on the other side of the river.

The river was clear and smoothly fast in the early morning. Down about two hundred yards were three logs all the way across the stream. They made the water smooth and deep above them. As Nick watched, a mink crossed the river on the logs and went into the swamp. Nick was excited. He was excited by the early morning and the river. He was really too hurried to eat breakfast, but he knew he must. He built a little fire and put on the coffee-pot.

While the water was heating in the pot he took an empty bottle and went down over the edge of the high ground to the meadow. The meadow was wet with dew and Nick wanted to catch grasshoppers for bait before the sun dried the grass. He found plenty of good grasshoppers. They were at the base of the grass stems. Sometimes they clung to a grass stem. They were cold and wet with the dew, and could not jump until the sun warmed them. Nick picked them up, taking only the medium-sized brown ones, and put them into the bottle. He turned over a log and just under the shelter of the edge were several hundred grasshoppers. It was a grasshopper lodging house. Nick put about fifty of the medium brown ones into the bottle. While he was picking up the hoppers the others warmed in the sun and commenced to hop away. They flew when they hopped. At first they made one flight and stayed stiff when they landed, as though they were dead.

Nick knew that by the time he was through with breakfast they would be as lively as ever. Without dew on the grass it would take him all day to catch a bottle full of good grass-hoppers and he would have to crush many of them, slamming at them with his hat. He washed his hands at the stream. He was excited to be near it. Then he walked up to the tent. The hoppers were already jumping stiffly in the grass. In the bottle, warmed by the sun, they were jumping in a mass. Nick put in a pine stick as a cork. It plugged the mouth of the bottle enough, so the hoppers could not get out and left plenty of air passage.

He had rolled the log back and knew he could get grasshoppers there every morning.

Nick laid the bottle full of jumping grasshoppers against a pine trunk. Rapidly he mixed some buckwheat flour with water and stirred it smooth, one cup of flour, one cup of water. He put a handful of coffee in the pot and dipped a lump of grease out of a can and slid it sputtering across the hot skillet. On the smoking skillet he poured smoothly the buckwheat batter. It spread like lava, the grease spitting sharply. Around the edges the buckwheat cake began to firm, then brown, then crisp. The surface was bubbling slowly to porousness. Nick pushed under the browned under surface with a fresh pine chip. He shook the skillet sideways and the cake was loose on the surface. I won't try and flop it, he thought. He slid the chip of clean wood all the way under the cake, and flopped it over on to its face. It sputtered in the pan.

When it was cooked Nick regreased the skillet. He used all the batter. It made another big flapjack and one smaller one.

Nick ate a big flapjack and a smaller one, covered with apple butter. He put apple butter on the third cake, folded it over twice, wrapped it in oiled paper, and put it in his shirt pocket. He put the apple-butter jar back in the pack and cut bread for two sandwiches.

In the pack he found a big onion. He sliced it in two and peeled the silky outer skin. Then he cut one half into slices and made onion sandwiches. He wrapped them in oiled paper and buttoned them in the other pocket of his khaki shirt. He turned the skillet upside down on the grill, drank the coffee, sweetened and yellow brown with the condensed milk in it, and tidied up the camp. It was a good camp.

Nick took his fly rod out of the leather rod-case, jointed it, and shoved the rod-case back into the tent. He put on the reel and threaded the line through the guides. He had to hold it from hand to hand, as he threaded it, or it would slip back through its own weight. It was a heavy, double-tapered fly line. Nick had paid eight dollars for it a long time ago. It was made

128

heavy to lift back in the air and come forward flat and heavy and straight to make it possible to cast a fly which had no weight. Nick opened the aluminium leader box. The leaders were coiled between the damp flannel pads. Nick had wet the pads at the water cooler on the train up to St Ignace. In the damp pads the gut leaders had softened and Nick unrolled one and tied it by a loop at the end of the heavy fly line. He fastened a hook on the end of the leader. It was a small hook; very thin and springy.

Nick took it from his hook book, sitting with the rod across his lap. He tested the knot and the spring of the rod by pulling the line taut. It was a good feeling. He was careful not to let the hook bite into his finger.

He started down to the stream, holding his rod, the bottle of grasshoppers hung from his neck by a thong tied in half hitches around the neck of the bottle. His landing-net hung by a hook from his belt. Over his shoulder was a long flour sack tied at each corner into an ear. The cord went over his shoulder. The sack flapped against his legs.

Nick felt awkward and professionally happy with all his equipment hanging from him. The grasshopper bottle swung against his chest. In his shirt the breast pockets bulged against him with the lunch and his fly book.

He stepped into the stream. It was a shock. His trousers clung tight to his legs. His shoes felt the gravel. The water was a rising cold shock.

Rushing, the current sucked against his legs. Where he stepped in, the water was over his knees. He waded with the current. The gravel slid under his shoes. He looked down at the swirl of water below each leg and tipped up the bottle to get a grasshopper.

The first grasshopper gave a jump in the neck of the bottle and went out into the water. He was sucked under in the whirl by Nick's right leg and came to the surface a little way downstream. He floated rapidly, kicking. In a quick circle, breaking the smooth surface of the water, he disappeared. A trout had taken him.

Another hopper poked his face out of the bottle. His antennae wavered. He was getting his front legs out of the bottle to jump. Nick took him by the head and held him while he threaded the slim hook under his chin, down through his thorax and into the last segments of his abdomen. The grass-hopper took hold of the hook with his front feet, spitting tobacco juice on it. Nick dropped him into the water.

Holding the rod in his right hand he let out line against the pull of the grasshopper in the current. He stripped off line from the reel with his left hand and let it run free. He could see the hopper in the little waves of the current. It went out of sight.

There was a tug on the line. Nick pulled against the taut line. It was his first strike. Holding the now living rod across the currents, he brought in the line with his left hand. The rod bent in jerks, the trout pumping against the current. Nick knew it was a small one. He lifted the rod straight up in the air. It bowed with the pull.

He saw the trout in the water jerking with his head and body against the shifting tangent of the line in the stream.

Nick took the line in his left hand and pulled the trout, thumping tiredly against the current, to the surface. His back was mottled the clear, water-over-gravel colour, his side flashing in the sun. The rod under his right arm, Nick stooped, dipping his right hand into the current. He held the trout, never still, with his moist right hand, while he unhooked the barb from his mouth, then dropped him back into the stream.

He hung unsteadily in the current, then settled to the bottom beside a stone. Nick reached down his hand to touch him, his arm to the elbow under water. The trout was steady in the moving stream, resting on the gravel, beside a stone. As Nick's fingers touched him, touched his smooth, cool, underwater feeling he was gone, gone in a shadow across the bottom of the stream.

He's all right, Nick thought. He was only tired.

He had wet his hand before he touched the trout, so he would not disturb the delicate mucus that covered him. If a trout was touched with a dry hand, a white fungus attacked the unprotected spot. Years before when he had fished crowded streams, with fly fishermen ahead of him and behind him, Nick had again and again come on dead trout, furry with white fungus, drifted against a rock, or floating belly-up in some

130

pool. Nick did not like to fish with other men on the river. Unless they were of your party, they spoiled it.

He wallowed down the stream, above his knees in the current, through the fifty yards of shallow water above the pile of logs that crossed the stream. He did not rebait his hook and held it in his hand as he waded. He was certain he could catch small trout in the shallows, but he did not want them. There would be no big trout in the shallows this time of day.

Now the water deepened up his thighs sharply and coldly. Ahead was the smooth damned-back flood of water above the logs. The water was smooth and dark; on the left, the lower edge of the meadow; on the right the swamp.

Nick leaned back against the current and took a hopper from the bottle. He threaded the hopper on the hook and spat on him for good luck. Then he pulled several yards of line from the reel and tossed the hopper out ahead on to the fast, dark water. It floated down towards the logs, then the weight of the line pulled the bait under the surface. Nick held the rod in his right hand, letting the line run out through his fingers.

There was a long tug. Nick struck and the rod came alive and dangerous, bent double, the line tightening, coming out of water, tightening, all in a heavy, dangerous, steady pull. Nick felt the moment when the leader would break if the strain increased and let the line go.

The reel ratcheted into a mechanical shriek as the line went out in a rush. Too fast. Nick could not check it, the line rushing out, the reel note rising as the line ran out.

With the core of the reel showing, his heart feeling stopped with the excitement, leaning back against the current that mounted icily his thighs, Nick thumbed the reel hard with his left hand. It was awkward getting his thumb inside the fly reel frame.

As he put on pressure the line tightened into sudden hardness and beyond the logs a huge trout went high out of water. As he jumped, Nick lowered the tip of the rod. But he felt, as he dropped the tip to ease the strain, the moment when the strain was too great; the hardness too tight. Of course, the leader was broken. There was no mistaking the feeling when all spring had left the line and it became dry and hard. Then it went slack.

His mouth dry, his heart down, Nick reeled in. He had never seen so big a trout. There was a heaviness, a power not to be held, and then the bulk of him, as he jumped. He looked as broad as a salmon.

Nick's hand was shaky. He reeled in slowly. The thrill had been too much. He felt, vaguely, a little sick, as though it would be better to sit down.

The leader had broken where the hook was tied to it. Nick took it in his hand. He thought of the trout somewhere on the bottom, holding himself steady over the gravel, far down below the light, under the logs, with the hook in his jaw. Nick knew the trout's teeth would cut through the snell of the hook. The hook would imbed itself in his jaw. He'd bet the trout was angry. Anything that size would be angry. That was a trout. He had been solidly hooked. Solid as a rock. He felt like a rock, too, before he started off. By God, he was a big one. By God, he was the biggest one I ever heard of.

Nick climbed out on to the meadow and stood, water running down his trousers and out of his shoes, his shoes squelchy. He went over and sat on the logs. He did not want to rush his sensations any.

He wriggled his toes in the water, in his shoes, and got out a cigarette from his breast pocket. He lit it and tossed the match into the fast water below the logs. A tiny trout rose at the match, as it swung around in the fast current. Nick laughed. He would finish the cigarette.

He sat on the logs, smoking, drying in the sun, the sun warm on his back, the river shallow ahead entering the woods, curving into the woods, shallows, light glittering, big water-smooth rocks, cedars along the bank and white birches, the logs warm in the sun, smooth to sit on, without bark, grey to the touch; slowly the feeling of disappointment left him. It went away slowly, the feeling of disappointment that came sharply after the thrill that made his shoulders ache. It was all right now. His rod lying out on the logs, Nick tied a new hook on the leader, pulling the gut tight until it grimped into itself in a hard knot.

He baited it, then picked up the rod and walked to the far end of the logs to get into the water, where it was not too deep.

Under and beyond the logs was a deep pool. Nick walked around the shallow shelf near the swamp shore until he came out on the shallow bed of the stream.

On the left, where the meadow ended and the woods began a great elm tree was uprooted. Gone over in a storm, it lay back into the woods, its roots clotted with dirt, grass growing in them, rising a solid bank beside the stream. The river cut to the edge of the uprooted tree. From where Nick stood he could see deep channels, like ruts, cut in the shallow bed of the stream by the flow of the current. Pebbly where he stood and pebbly and full of boulders beyond; where it curved near the tree roots, the bed of the stream was marly and between the ruts of deep water green weed fronds swung in the current.

Nick swung the rod back over his shoulder and forward, and the line, curving forward, laid the grasshopper down on one of the deep channels in the weeds. A trout struck and Nick hooked him.

Holding the rod far out toward the uprooted tree and sloshing backward in the current, Nick worked the trout, plunging, the rod bending alive, out of the danger of the weeds into the open river. Holding the rod, pumping alive against the current, Nick brought the trout in. He rushed, but always came, the spring of the rod yielding to the rushes, sometimes jerking under the water, but always bringing him in. Nick eased downstream with the rushes. The rod above his head he led the trout over the net, then lifted.

The trout hung heavy in the net, mottled trout back and silver sides in the meshes. Nick unhooked him, heavy sides, good to hold, big undershot jaw, and slipped him, heaving and big sliding, into the long sack that hung from his shoulders in the water.

Nick spread the mouth of the sack against the current and it filled, heavy with water. He held it up, the bottom in the stream, and the water poured out through the sides. Inside at the bottom was the big trout, alive in the water.

Nick moved downstream. The sack out ahead of him sunk heavy in the water, pulling from his shoulders.

It was getting hot, the sun hot on the back of his neck.

Nick had one good trout. He did not care about getting

133

many trout. Now the stream was shallow and wide. There were trees along both banks. The trees of the left bank made short shadows on the current in the forenoon sun. Nick knew there were trout in each shadow. In the afternoon, after the sun had crossed toward the hills, the trout would be in the cool shadows on the other side of the stream.

The very biggest ones would lie up close to the bank. You could always pick them up there on the Black. When the sun was down they all moved out into the current. Just when the sun made the water blinding in the glare before it went down, you were liable to strike a big trout anywhere in the current. It was almost impossible to fish then, the surface of the water was blinding as a mirror in the sun. Of course, you could fish upstream, but in a stream like the Black, or this, you had to wallow against the current, and, in a deep place, the water piled up on you. It was no fun to fish upstream with this much current.

Nick moved along through the shallow stretch watching the banks for deep holes. A beech tree grew close beside the river, so that the branches hung down into the water. The stream went back in under the leaves. There were always trout in a place like that.

Nick did not care about fishing that hole. He was sure he would get hooked in the branches.

It looked deep though. He dropped the grasshopper so the current took it under water, back in under the overhanging branch. The line pulled hard and Nick struck The trout threshed heavily, half out of the water in the leaves and branches. The line was caught. Nick pulled hard and the trout was off. He reeled in and, holding the hook in his hand, walked down the stream.

Ahead, close to the left bank, was a big log. Nick saw it was hollow; pointing up river the current entered it smoothly, only a little ripple spread each side of the log. The water was deepening. The top of the hollow log was grey and dry. It was partly in the shadow.

Nick took the cork out of the grasshopper bottle and a hopper clung to it. He picked him off, hooked him, and tossed him out. He held the rod far out so that the hopper on the water moved into the current flowing into the hollow log. Nick lowered the rod and the hopper floated in. There was a heavy strike. Nick swung the rod against the pull. It felt as though he were hooked into the log itself, except for the live feeling.

He tried to force the fish out into the current. It came, heavily.

The line went slack, and Nick thought the trout was gone. Then he saw him, very near, in the current, shaking his head trying to get the hook out. His mouth was clamped shut. He was fighting the hook in the clear flowing current.

Looping the line with his left hand, Nick swung the rod to make the line taut and tried to lead the trout toward the net, but he was gone, out of sight, the line pumping. Nick fought him against the current, letting him thump in the water against the spring of the rod. He shifted the rod to his left hand, worked the trout upstream, holding his weight, fighting on the rod, and then let him down into the net. He lifted him clear of the water, a heavy half circle in the net, the net dripping, unhooked him and slid him into the sack.

He spread the mouth of the sack and looked down in at the two big trout alive in the water.

Through the deepening water, Nick waded over to the hollow log. He took the sack off, over his head, the trout flopping as it came out of the water, and hung it so the trout were deep in the water. Then he pulled himself up on the log and sat, the water from his trousers and boots running down in the stream. He laid his rod down, moved along to the shady end of the log, and took the sandwiches out of his pocket. He dipped the sandwiches in the cold water. The current carried away the crumbs. He ate the sandwiches and dipped his hat full of water to drink, the water running out through his hat just ahead of his drinking.

It was cool in the shade, sitting on the log. He took a cigarette out and struck a match to light it. The match sunk into the grey wood, making a tiny furrow. Nick leaned over the side of the log, found a hard place, and lit the match. He sat smoking and watching the river.

Ahead the river narrowed and went into a swamp. The river

became smooth and deep and the swamp looked solid with cedar trees, their trunks close together, their branches solid. It would not be possible to walk through a swamp like that. The branches grew so low. You would have to keep almost level with the ground to move at all. You could not crash through the branches. That must be why the animals that lived in swamps were built the way they were, Nick thought.

He wished he had brought something to read. He felt like reading. He did not feel like going on into the swamp. He looked down the river. A big cedar slanted all the way across the stream. Beyond that the river went into the swamp.

Nick did not want to go in there now. He felt a reaction against deep wading with the water deepening up under his armpits, to hook big trout in places impossible to land them. In the swamp the banks were bare, the big cedars came together overhead, the sun did not come through, except in patches; in the fast deep water, in the half light, the fishing would be tragic. In the swamp, fishing was a tragic adventure. Nick did not want it. He did not want to go down the stream any farther today.

He took out his knife, opened it, and stuck it in the log. Then he pulled up the sack, reached into it, and brought out one of the trout. Holding him near the tail, hard to hold, alive, in his hand, he whacked him against the log. The trout quivered, rigid. Nick laid him on the log in the shade and broke the neck of the other fish the same way. He laid them side by side on the log. They were fine trout.

Nick cleaned them, slitting them from the vent to the tip of the jaw. All the insides and the gills and tongue came out in one piece. They were both males; long grey-white strips of milt, smooth and clean. All the insides clean and compact, coming out all together. Nick tossed the offal ashore for the minks to find.

He washed the trout in the stream. When he held them back up in the water they looked like live fish. Their colour was not gone yet. He washed his hands and dried them on the log. Then he laid the trout on the sack spread out on the log, rolled them up in it, tied the bundle, and put it in the landing-net. His knife was still standing, blade stuck in the log. He cleaned it on the wood and put it in his pocket.

Nick stood up on the log, holding his rod, the landing-net hanging heavy, then stepped into the water and splashed ashore. He climbed the bank and cut up into the woods, toward the high ground. He was going back to camp. He looked back. The river just showed through the trees. There were plenty of days coming when he could fish the swamps.